VACCINATION

PHILLIP TOMASSO

This one is for my family at 911;
to the Telecomunicators who take calls;
to the Fire, EMS and Police Dispatchers who tell responders where to
go!

Love All of You.

Thank you for the inspiration!

PROLOGUE

Chris Danson stared at the male who stood motionless more than halfway down the liquor store's first aisle. The guy's disheveled hair looked wet and matted down against his scalp; the black suit, wrinkled.

"Anything I can help you with?" Behind the counter Danson leaned on the heel of his hands.

The guy looked up. First thing Danson noticed were bloodshot eyes—must have been on an all-morning bender.

"Buddy, something I can give you a hand with?"

The guy turned with his whole body, faced Danson. The knot on the black necktie hung low against his chest and the un-tucked white dress shirt appeared as if a red pen exploded in the breast pocket.

"You're going to have to get out of here." Danson shook his head. "I'm not going to be able to sell you anything. And man, buddy, you're drooling all over the floor."

The slow staggered steps only reassured Danson the right decision had been made. "You're gonna have to leave. I want you out of my store. Okay?"

Danson worked alone most days from open until roughly six or seven. Aside from the handful of customers who religiously kept to liquid lunch diets, the low volume didn't warrant anyone else on the clock. It was early evenings when things became hectic. Like, people left work and needed a bottle more than dinner, and for whatever reasons, had to have it before heading home. That's when it made sense to have extra help on hand. But not now. Not at eleven in the morning.

"Sir, I don't want trouble, okay? But I'm thinking, if you don't just leave, I'm going to have to call the police. Look, it's not something I want to do, all right? So, what'd ya say? Don't make me do that." Danson held up his cell phone, if only to show the threat of meaning business.

The guy's expression did not change—at all. But neither did he look right. Not right at all. Danson shook his head, shrugged, and walked around to the front of the counter, then with long strides toward the first aisle, mentally preparing to throw the drunk out physically, if warranted.

When he rounded the front of the aisle, he stopped short. "Shit!"

The guy stood there, face-to-face. The bloodshot eyes were nothing compared to the pulsing blue veins that appeared almost neon under dead-gray flesh. Danson jumped back a step, and thought, *Maybe he was just going to leave.*

"Okay, sir. I do appreciate your business. Normally. Tell you what, you come back when you are a little more sober. I'll give you a special on whatever you pick out. How's that sound?"

Then Danson did something, and knew the moment that he did, he shouldn't have. He turned his back on the oddball customer, with the intent of opening the front door and hoping the messed up guy would leave.

He wouldn't have said he'd expected hands to grab his shoulders, but when it happened, he wasn't surprised. What shocked him most was the bite.

Teeth dug into the nape of his neck, scraped across what felt like his spine, and tore out chunks of meat from his shoulder. Screaming and attempting to reach up and over his shoulder to pull the guy's head off his neck, was as futile as reaching around to remove a knife from the center of one's own back.

# # #

"Hey, man, you got like, what, five bucks?" Josh shut the engine off and the car stopped alongside the pump.

"Six." David moved his hand around the seat belt, and dug fingertips into pants pockets and spider-walked out crumpled bills. "Ah, um, four. I have four dollars."

Josh rolled his eyes. "Four? Seriously? Four?"

"I thought I had six," he said.

Josh climbed out of the car, but not before tossing over a ten. "Go pay. All fourteen. Got it?"

With the cap unscrewed, the nozzle buried in the tank, Josh watched for the gas pump to switch on. While waiting, he saw the woman in the jean skirt and tank top across the street from the gas station. Long legs. Blonde hair. With his back to his car, he could stare all he wanted. It only looked like he was watching gauges on a pump.

"Damn," he said.

"You're good, dude, you're good. Go ahead and pump."

Josh spun around.

David stepped out from between the pumps, toward the car.

"What's that?" Josh hated that he usually had to ask everything twice, and even then, twice rarely seemed to sink in with David.

"A Slim Jim."

"You had four dollars for me, but enough for a Slim Jim," Josh asked.

"Actually, I used *our* money. Just a dollar for the Slim Jim."

"Do you not understand, we're broke and need gas?"

He pulled a second Slim Jim out of his back pocket, and held it out like a magic wand. "Ah, but Bro—I got one for you, too!"

Josh moaned. David didn't get it. Just could not comprehend the concept of *broke*. "Get in the car. You know what, just get in the car."

"Whoa! What she doing?"

The blonde in the short skirt walked into traffic. Not at the crosswalk, and with no regard for vehicles headed at her from both directions. Rubber bled like black white-out across the pavement, as tires screamed in protest; horns like sirens from the Ginna Nuclear Power Plant, blared in long, relentless blasts.

"Hey! Hey, watch out!" Josh called.

The woman slowly crossed the lanes, walked with a limp, and seemed more focused on Josh and David than her personal safety.

"She crippled, or what?"

"No idea," Josh said. "Hurt, maybe. She looks hurt."

"And mental. It's like, what could she be thinking?"

Josh took a step toward the woman and shook off the hand that reached for his arm. "She don't look well. Maybe call nine-one-one."

"You think?"

The closer Josh got, the more he thought she wasn't looking at him, but that she might be blind. Both eyes looked milky, grayish, and white. Not the pupil. No eye color at all, just a milky grayish-white. It explained her walking across lanes of traffic without looking in any direction first, or during. She'd have to be deaf, too. The screech of tires, honking horns. "Ma'am? Ah, Miss?"

"Call? Should I call, Josh?"

"I think we're going to need an ambulance. Something messed up happened to this woman," Josh said. He whispered, thinking she couldn't hear him, but just in case. "Look at her foot. She's walking on a broken ankle."

"So call?"

"Yeah, man. Call."

"What do I tell them?"

Josh was less than ten feet from the woman. He saw scratch marks that started at her neck and seemed to slide down to between her breasts. There were more on her thighs. The ankle wasn't just broken. The foot merely hung on by threads of flesh and meat. She walked on the compound fracture without wincing. "Tell them to get an ambulance and the police here. Both, she needs both. Someone fucked her up, bad. I mean, she's all fucked up."

Josh grabbed the woman gently by the shoulders. She stared right at him, as if she could see him, but like she saw right through him. Vision had to be impossible. It looked like congealed fat on a piece of chuck roast left in the fridge overnight and had hardened over her eyeballs.

When she tried to bite him, arms flailed, he did not take it personal. "It's going to be all right. We've got help on the way, ma'am. Okay? An ambulance is coming."

As gently as possible, Josh got alongside the woman and lowered her to the pavement. She fought him, but without much effort. She may have been walking for miles. Her skin was cold, no fever, but shock could be infecting her. "Get me a blanket from the trunk. David? A blanket. Get one from the trunk."

"I'm on the line with nine-one-one," he said.

"Do two things at once, asshole!" Josh loved his kid brother, but damn him sometimes. Damn him.

The woman bucked, arching her back. She coughed, gagged. Josh rolled her onto her side, so she faced away from him. He didn't want her to choke on vomit or her tongue, or anything, but neither did he want to watch her if she did. She blows chunks; he's going to be blowing chunkier chunks right along with her.

"I got the blanket."

"Cover her legs."

"What about the blood?"

"Seriously? Cover her legs, please!" Josh grunted. He would have yanked the blanket away and covered the woman himself, but she still twisted, tried rolling over, or getting up. Josh had no idea what she was trying to do. He didn't want to let go of her shoulders and risk letting her cause more damage. "*They* sending an ambulance?"

"They said they were and they asked me a million questions. I didn't know how to answer any of them. Felt stupid. Had to keep saying, 'I don't know.'"

Yeah. That's what made you feel stupid. "The police?"

"I guess they're coming, too."

"They say how long?" Josh made sure the blanket covered her legs. He stretched it as far up to her lower chest as he could without leaving bare skin exposed. It was October. Not freezing out, but too cold to be in a short skirt and tank top. "Give me your coat, David."

"My coat, Josh?"

"Your coat. I want to cover her shoulders."

"What about your coat?"

"I'm wearing mine," Josh said.

David hugged himself; his fingers ran over his arms. "It's in the car."

Distant sirens.

"Okay. Can you get it, David? Can you, please, just fucking go and get it?"

David stared off into the distance. "Could be them?"

"Could be. She still needs your coat." Josh looked up and down the main road. He thought the sirens got closer, but couldn't yet see the responders. "I have a feeling she's not going to make it."

"Dude, she looks dead already."

Josh could only nod. No argument. She did indeed look dead.

CHAPTER ONE

"Chase, you know it's not *your* Halloween this year. It's mine."

Just the sound of her voice ate through me. Thank God, we were on phones, not talking in person. The urge to clock her made my bicep muscle twitch instinctively. "Look, Julie. Charlene is fourteen. Cash is nine. They aren't going to want to go trick or treating much longer. All I am saying is, let me go around with them. A couple of houses. You and Douglas—"

"Donald."

"—can stay home and hand out candy. You don't want to leave a mini mansion like that unattended on a night like that anyway." That was thoughtful of me. Worrying about the safety of Dougla— Donald's—possessions, expensive possessions. At least I thought so.

"Chase, we're not doing this. You had them last year. I didn't do this to you. I didn't call and beg to impose. I will send you pictures of them in their costumes."

"They're my kids, Julie. I'm not imposing if I want to spend time with *my* kids." I lit a cigarette. My morning cup of coffee forgotten, gone cold, sat next to the butt-full ashtray.

"I'm hanging up now."

"I hate that. You know I hate that."

"Can you guess what's great about being divorced from you? I don't care what you hate."

"See, you can't do that. You can't ask me to guess and then just give the answer. I need a chance actually to guess."

"Fine. You know what, from now on, to make it easier for you, I won't tell you when I—"

The line disconnected.

"You hang up on me? Jules? Julie?" I threw my phone, pissed off enough to aim for a wall, but broke enough to ensure it slammed into a couch cushion instead. I leaned back in the wood chair, but not so far that the legs might snap. Because they might. The square card table was dressed up with a kitchen-like tablecloth and surrounded with a mismatch of chairs. Curb side furniture.

Smoke billowed up from the end of my cigarette, hit the yellow stained ceiling paint and burst like a silent exploding cloud. I shook my head. Thirty-five, divorced, not where I saw myself.

Work and beer when not working. Killing days until my every-other-weekend, and one day a week with my kids. *She* cheated. She forced me out. She got the kids. Courts favored mothers.

I fought. At first.

Whole time we were together I promised her, if anything ever happened to us, I was taking the kids. Her boyfriend at the time hired an expensive firm. The only way I'd win in court was airing laundry in front of a judge, and dragging my kids through the stink.

That didn't help them. The kids. I made it about them. She made it about winning. Rough enough having their parents split. They didn't need to testify and choose sides. She was prepared to put them through that. Not me. I walked away.

One day, I told myself, they'd know I didn't give up. I sacrificed . . . for them. It's always been for them.

The phone chirped; it was a text. I turned and parted the kitchen curtain and watched the rain as it fell. Not heavy. Gray clouds covered any sunlight. It was the end of October and I might not see sunlight until March. I worked from four in the afternoon, until midnight. Got home. Got drunk. Passed out. Woke up, usually around now—which was what? Two? Showered and headed back into work.

We were coming up on the weekend, the busiest time at work and it would be ten times worse this weekend, because it was Halloween weekend. Years when the holiday fell on a school night, things were better. There were fewer parties and fewer drunks. Not a lot less. But fewer.

I stood up, pushed in my chair, set the cigarette down in the ashtray, and retrieved my phone.

Allison. Entered my password. Read the message.

As I walked back for my smoke, I spoke my reply. "Reply. Hey, dear. Getting ready for work. You want coffee? See you there. Send."

I set the phone down and walked toward the bathroom.

The scream came from outside my door. I stopped. Listened. Eyes narrowed, like that helped my ears. It didn't.

A moan. Loud. Long. I back stepped through the living room, and pressed my ear to the apartment door, straining to listen.

Nothing. Silence.

I waited.

I had been living in this building for close to a year. I said hello and goodbye to the other tenants, but little else. I wasn't here to make friends. I needed a place to sleep, and drink, and it worked fine for my purposes.

When several minutes passed without another sound from the hallway, I walked past the television. A news journalist reviewed the shortness of H7N9 vaccinations, and the alarmingly large number of U.S. citizens infected with the fast-spreading flu. I would take my chances. Saw no reason to stop for a flu shot. Never got one before, and wasn't getting one now.

At the table, I crushed out the butt, lit a fresh smoke and went to the bathroom to shower. I'd grab hot coffee at the drive-thru and head into work.

Work was not solace. It was a place that kept me sober eight hours at a time. You might consider 9-1-1 a sanctuary. Unless you worked there. Then you'd know it was more like a detention center. A holding cell for the mentally employed, and moderately deranged. I fit the mold. Explained why I still had a job.

CHAPTER TWO

Allison Little answered on the second ring. "Hello, Chase."

"Hey," I said. Idling in line at Tim Horton's, I fished out my wallet without unfastening my seat belt. With the windows down, the cigarette smoke mostly escaped in slow billowing plumes. "I'm getting coffee. You didn't answer. You need anything?"

"Hot tea?"

"Three sugars. No cream."

"See you at work?"

"Be there in a few."

"I just walked in. People are ordered." She sighed. "Four. Four people ordered."

When someone called in sick, people working on the ending shift were forced to stay. They called it Getting Ordered. It was time and a half, but no one was ever happy about it. A sixteen-hour shift sucked. Though no one admitted it, there had to be liability issues. I've learned to keep my mouth shut and cause as few waves as possible, fly as low under the radar as I can, and whatever other clichés fit the situation. "Probably be more orders in the morning, too."

Unfortunately, calling in sick was sometimes the only way to get time off. No one wanted to see other employees ordered, but mental health days were essential at times. The good thing, once ordered, you moved to the bottom of the list. If you were lucky, you might get ordered four to six times a year. If you were lucky, that is.

"I'm going to stop at the drugstore after work," she said. I heard the hesitant tone of her voice. She knew I'd not received a shot, and maybe she thought I'd be upset that she planned to. I didn't give a fuck.

"The shot?"

"I can't afford to get the flu," she said, "you know that."

"That's cool," I said, because, really, what else was there to say? I knew she was asking without asking, if I wanted to go. I didn't. Not interested. "I'll see you soon." I ended the call, eased up my car up to the box, stopped, and ordered.

# # #

Headed south on Lake Avenue, I shook my head. It was just after 3 P.M. The streets seemed excessively crowded, not with cars, but people. It was usually on my way home at midnight that I had to be extra cautious. City residents crossed the streets without looking. They walked on the roads as if they owned them. Dressed in dark clothing, they often times looked like the pavement. Blended. It annoyed me. I never slowed. Screw them. Eventually, they hurried across. They'd flip me off, but that didn't concern me. I'd flip them off right back.

Today, groups seemed to linger, almost mingling in the middle of the road. They moved at a sluggish pace. Dragging their feet, literally. Honking my horn did little to hurry them along. Gritting my teeth, I was forced to serpentine through the growing mass. Veering left and right, as if on a crazy course where orange pylons were replaced with humans.

As I crossed Driving Park, I checked my rear-view mirror to see how cars behind me fared. One car had stopped. Bad idea. The crowd that meandered, converged. Not a good sign. Stopping is like asking for trouble, as if you had thrown down a challenge. Unless the guy driving is illegally packing, he might be in for some shit he never expected.

I looked forward, watched where I was going. Someone would call work, 9-1-1. Someone always did. Not me. It wasn't my business, and as far as I was concerned, the person in the stopped car brought any trouble received on himself.

When I got to work, I'd type in the inner section, Lake and Driving, and see if a job was put in, check out what ended up happening, if anything. Figure by the time police are dispatched, the group will have dispersed anyway. They smelled the police. Knew when to scatter. Knew there would never be a witness. Not one who would talk, help the police out.

Every generation comes to a point where they claim the end of the world has got to be just around the corner. I was in my mid-thirties, certain and confident it was just a matter of time. Things were coming to a head: rising gas prices, increased backward leaps in racism, segregation, political angst, infringement on nearly every point of the Constitution by the president, and just an overall sense of angry people. It was hard not to read the graffiti on the walls around us. If you couldn't see it, if you didn't sense it, then I guess you were just a blind motherfucker living under some rock.

Aside from the amblers in the street, traffic itself seemed light. I zipped down Lake Ave to West and turned up the volume on the radio. Bass thumped. Singer screamed. Guitars like sirens blared. I nearly closed my eyes, soothed by the frantic chaos of rhythm exploding from my speakers.

I lit a cigarette, inhaled deeply. As smoke filled my lungs, damaged arteries, messed up what was left of the muscle that was my beating heart, I smiled and exhaled slowly. A calm enveloping my senses. It wouldn't last. The calm. One puff at a time. There really wasn't any other way to continue, was there?

Once I pulled into the parking lot at work, I felt it. The tightness in my chest. It did not come from smoking. It came from stress. I didn't want to be here. I'm not sure I'd want to be at work at any job, but here? Completely unique kind of *I-don't-want-to-be-here* sense of overbearing dread. Trust me.

Political bullshit reigned. Backstabbing, lunch stealing, whining teenage-like drama, cliques, bullies (both peer-related, and supervisor enforced), hostile, harassing, sexual charged atmosphere. 9-1-1 was like a high school, with less mature employees. If they couldn't find something to bitch about, they manufactured things. But who respected upper management?

The place reminded me of that scene in *Willy Wonka and the Chocolate Factory*, where Wonka handed out the ever-desired Everlasting Gobstopper to the Golden Ticket toting winners. One for each kid. Of course, Slugworth had bribed each child with untold riches prior to the factory tour if they would part with their single piece of candy. Veruca Salt, stingy bastard that she was, tried to get two. Why? So she could keep one, and sell one. *Bitch.*

Of course, I'm referring to the original. With Gene Wilder. Not the lame re-make with Depp. I like Depp. Don't get me wrong. However, that rendition was totally spoiled by the single Umpa-Lumpa multiplied by however many in computer graphics. Awful.

I shut the engine, and finally took a few seconds just to close my eyes.

A futile attempt to obtain one last moment of solitude. It's what I needed. Then, exhaling like a quick-deflating zeppelin, I headed in.

CHAPTER THREE

My shift started at four. I checked out the schedule thumbtacked to the cork. I'm normally a dispatcher, sending fire trucks and ambulances to emergency calls. Police dispatchers worked the opposite side of the room. Between the two sets of dispatchers, sat telecommunications. The call takers. The 9-1-1 Operators. These are the unsung heroes of the place. The hub of the operation. They take call after call after belligerent call. I don't know how they do it. Night after night. God bless them.

Tonight, I had phones. It's a blessing and a curse. As a dispatcher, I am required to answer phones once every five to six days. I'd rather answer phone calls tonight, in the middle of the week, than on a weekend. Luckily, this year, I had Halloween off. Phones on a holiday, any holiday, were the definition of a nightmare. Families spending time together never ended well. Families hated each other, I've learned. However, tradition forced them to break bread umpteen times a year.

The curse, anyway, being that regardless of *when*, I sucked on phones. You never know what's waiting on the other end of each ring. We're trained to be ready. Graded on it, and disciplined from it.

I rounded the corner. Allison Little. She sat at one of the four round tables in the break room. Flat screen TV was on, volume low.

She was an all right girlfriend, seemed to love me. Which was cool. No complaint with that. For the most part, I tolerated her. Wish it could be more. After six months, should be more, I guess. Wasn't though.

Her shoulder length blonde hair looked cute when she wore it pulled back in a tight ponytail--as she wore it tonight. Her bright, blue eyes always looked happy. Can't think of a better word. They Sparkled? They shined? The girl was twenty-seven. Never married. Still thought life was some peach, a glorified bed of roses, and she acted as if she'd just seductively wait in it for her knight to show up and validate some fabled fairytale story of her life.

Nearly impossible at times not to grab and shake her by the shoulders, and yell, "Wake the fuck up!"

"Got your tea." I set the cup down in front of her.

I kissed the top of her head and sat down next to her.

"Thank you," she said. I guess I liked the way she smiled, too. Coupled with those eyes, yeah, I'd say she was very attractive. Think what I hated most was talking to her on the phone. Took a while to get her to understand that. I had no problem texting and shit. I just didn't want to talk. It's a simple concept. Women just seem flustered by it. Thing was, I was single more than in a relationship since my divorce. So maybe it was me. Don't know if that's a question though. Might be more of a statement. Maybe it was me.

I pulled the lid off my coffee. I picked up the sugar dispenser and dumped more into my cup, took a sip and smacked my lips. "That's good."

"See the schedule?"

"Phones."

"Me, too," she said. "We're in different pods, though."

"On purpose, no doubt," I shrugged. We were used to it. Could make an unbearable night more bearable working in pods where you didn't absolutely hate the people around you. See, that might improve morale, cause employees to feel valued. Just another way management was fucking with you. Everyone knew Allison and I were together. Some thought it was cool. Some simply displayed childish forms of jealousy. Dating co-workers wasn't prohibited as much as it was frowned upon. Thing was, we spent long, often difficult hours together. Relationships formed. Couldn't really be helped. Lot of people here were married. Many more dated, and it ended horribly. And, of course, there's the large handful of married (to non-employees) who dated peers, or just slept with them. I couldn't keep all the webs that linked everyone to everyone else straight. At some point, it just felt like Six Degrees of Kevin Bacon, anyway. I mean, who didn't love Bacon?

I needed another cigarette or two. Allison didn't smoke. Like talking on the phone, it took her a few weeks to learn not to give me shit about smoking. I smoked. She knew it when she met me. Magazines might give tips about how to change your man, but you know what? We don't change.

"I'll be back," I said, standing up. She smiled. Said nothing. Yeah, Allison was an all right girlfriend. I gave her a wink. "Did you see if we at least have breaks together or anything?"

"I'll check," she said.

"I got it. Look on my way out," I said.

CHAPTER FOUR

The *floor* is set up in pods. About thirty-five people work per shift. There are four different telecommunication pods, with four to five phone stations in each, a fire and ambulance dispatch pod with six stations, and lastly, two police dispatch pods for nine employees. There are people for breaks and lunch reliefs, and in the center of it all, three to four supervisors per shift oversee the night.

I logged on to the three terminals at my station, and plugged in my headset-jack. We're several calls in queue.

Allison stopped at the pod. "Putting me on the police side," she said.

"Lucky you." She sauntered away. I shook my head. Lucky her.

I made it through a handful of calls and sipped some water before answering the next.

"Nine-one-one Center," I said.

"Send an ambulance, please. Send an ambulance." It's a female voice.

I checked the left monitor. A landline. I have a name, address, and the number she's calling from. I still have to ask and verify. "What's your address, ma'am?"

"No," she yells. "No! Ah, God—he, he—"

"Ma'am, what is your address?" I filled out the electronic job template on the center monitor and brought the caller's information over with a keystroke. I heard crying, her sucking in gasps, and moaning. "Ma'am, I need your address."

It's the nature of the job. Night after night. No one ever knows where they are. If they do, I can rarely understand a word being said—what with crappy cell phone companies, and piss-poor annunciation. Landline calls were a bonus. There were far less of those calls, as people made cells their primary. I didn't have a home phone.

"He's sick. I mean, like really sick." I think she laughed. One of those nervous, anxious laughs. Not like something was funny, but like she was close to losing it.

"Where are you, ma'am?"

"He told me his toe itched. That it was itchy. And then, he, I—he—with the knife, he just cut it off."

"The toe?" I asked. I cocked my head to one side, and pressed a finger to my ear. Nothing should surprise me, but I thought, *I can't be hearing this right.*

"Where is the knife now?"

I'm closing in on two minutes since the start of the call. With no confirmed address, I'll need a supervisor's involvement. I hate that.

"Ma'am—"

She'd hung up.

I clicked on a button to dial her number. On the template I typed: F (for female) STATES M (for male) CUT OFF HIS TOE—M POSS (for possible) INTOX—CLR H/U (for caller hung up). It's all about short cuts and abbreviations. Get the job in, and the responders en route.

I transferred the address information I did have to the right-hand monitor, used for mapping.

On the third ring back, someone answered.

"This is nine-one-one. We were disconnected," I said.

Open line. Screaming in the background. Sounded like things being knocked over. Grunts, more groans.

A stifled scream?

I type: OPEN LINE ON C/B—HEAR SCREAMING, AND POSS STRUGGLE.

I had enough. I entered an event type for domestic dispute, and sent the job to the police dispatchers. I combined it with an ambulance job, who'll stage in the area until police cleared them in to the scene. If the guy cut off his toe, he was going to need medical attention for sure. For all I knew, by now, the female might as well.

The call disconnected. Dial tone hums.

As always, another call to be answered waited. No need to call the female back a second time. Police had the job. Someone would go, sort things out.

That training I told you about, taught us to move from call to call, not get hung up on what might, or might not be happening with the people involved in the last one. Not always easy to do. But after years employed here, it does become *robotically* automatic.

"Nine-one-one Center," I said, and looked up. There's flat screen TVs everywhere with subtitles, but no sound, and the only thing we're allowed to watch is news. I'm up to here with reality. News was the last thing I wanted to watch. Not to mention, reports mostly revolved around the H7N9 virus, and its vaccinations.

"Hello, this is nine-one-one," I said, again.

Open line.

Cell phone, this time. I re-bid the number—an attempt to triangulate the caller's location. Naturally, it's one of those cell phones you can get without a contract. They rarely work when doing this—trying to pin down the caller's location. These cell providers basically provide customers with junk phones at an affordable rate and piggyback off the more reputable service providers' towers.

The pictometry map refreshed, hit off a cell tower. I rebid again, just to be sure, and received the same cell tower. No location revealed.

The phones were useless.

I didn't hear anything in the background. After another thirty seconds, I release the call and try call back. It went to voice mail, and I disconnected. Nothing I could do. It was more than likely what we called a butt-dial. Happened all the time.

Twenty calls in queue. What the fuck?

# # #

"Nine-one-one Center."

"They're trying to get into my house!" Another female. On a cell. I rebid the call.

"What is your address ma'am? Ma'am?" I looked at pictometry. I got a street address. I rebid again. Same house. Same street.

"Please, please, send the police," she whispers.

"I need your address so I know where to send the police," I explained. Pictometry is helpful, but not a hundred-percent accurate.

She fed me an address. I'm surprised. She spoke slow and clear. I entered it. Verified it. It matched the mapping system. "Okay, tell me exactly what's going on?"

I filled out the text on the job template as she talked: 4 M'S TRYING TO BREAK INTO COMP'S HOUSE—BREAKING WINDOWS DOWNSTAIRS—COMP HIDING IN UPSTAIRS BEDROOM.

I have enough information. I plugged in a burglary-in-progress event type and sent the job.

Now I can supplement the job with additional information to keep responding police informed. "Do you know these men, ma'am?"

"No." The whisper is barely audible. "I'm under the bed now."

I typed that.

"Did you see them?"

"Yes."

"Were they white, black, or Hispanic?"

"It was too dark. I couldn't tell."

"Did you see what they were wearing?"

"They were covered in, I think they, it looked like they were covered in blood," she said.

"Blood?" I added that. 4 M'S POSS COVERED IN BLOOD. I sent the supplemental information, and got ready to add more. "Can you still hear them?"

"They broke my windows."

"Do you think they left?"

"I'm not going down to check!"

"No, ma'am. I don't want you to do that!" I pulled up the actual job on the bottom-half of the screen. Two police cars are en-route. "I want you to stay where you are. Stay on the phone with me. What's your name?"

My job now, calm the caller. Reassure her. I don't want to say police will be there any second. It doesn't always work that way. "Ma'am, what's your name?"

"Kenya."

"Okay, Kenya, did these men have any weapons?"

"I didn't see them with anything, but I don't know. I'm not sure."

"That's fine. That's okay. I'm just sharing all this information with the police, so they will know what to expect when they get there."

"Where are they?" She sounded worried. "I think they are inside the house."

SHE THINKS THEY ARE IN THE HOUSE NOW --sent the supplement.

"Does it sound like they're downstairs?"

"Can you hear them?" she asked.

I heard it. Groaning. Moaning. It's muffled. "Kenya?"

"They're outside my door."

I typed that. Sent it.

"Kenya, I want you to stay very quiet." I'm talking in a low voice, too. Hope that is calming. "But don't hang up. Keep the phone on. Okay?"

"Okay."

We're both quiet. I refreshed the job. Police on scene.

"Kenya, the police are outside. Don't move. Stay quiet."

I heard what had to be her bedroom door bang open. It's Kenya I heard next, screaming. Giving away her hiding spot. "Let go of me!"

"Kenya!"

I jumped up, faced the police dispatchers. It's a home invasion. "They have her!"

The line is still open. Screams echoed in my headset. I can't figure out the sounds. All I pictured is something like . . . pudding stirred in a bowl with a wood spoon, or mayonnaise into mac-salad. Wet, puckering. I have no idea what else describes the sounds I'm hearing.

"Where are they?" I yelled.

"They're in. They're in." Allison had the job and was on her feet, too. "Police are inside the house!"

"Police!" I heard from the headset.

Swearing. Must be the cops.

Kenya's screaming had stopped.

Gunshots.

"Shots fired," I yelled.

Allison and I, normally, would have the attention of everyone. I mean everyone if we'd yelled "shots fired" like that across the floor.

Tonight, no one noticed. Other employees had heads down, or were on their feet shouting, too. Only I was just noticing this. All the yelling. I'd been too caught up in Kenya's call.

Supervisors were in different pods, assisting. The Operations floor was in frenzied disarray.

It's a Tuesday. Rarely is it this busy unless it's summertime. Or like I've said, a holiday.

More than six hours left to go, I thought. I sit. Listen. Police have the scene. Nothing more I can do from here anyway. Despite being in queue, I am not going to disconnect the call. Not yet.

"Officers down," Allison yelled.

That did it. There was sudden silence, but it didn't last. But there it is. For just a moment *our* job captured every one's attention.

Supervisors had plenty to do when a responder was in trouble. Milzy rushed over to Allison.

Kenya's house would be swarming with cops.

"Kenya?" I said. "Hello?"

The struggle continued. All calls were recorded. A playback would be used in court. I'd have to testify. No way around it.

We're forty calls in queue. The number kept climbing. I'd never seen this before. Heard it happened once when a tiny earthquake shook part of the county with little more than patio furniture tipping over during the aftershock.

I logged the job number down on a pad so I could check on Kenya's situation later. I didn't want to hang up, but it truly was no longer my concern.

Again, just the way it was.

# # #

I took the next call, and thought, it's going to be one hell of a *Happy Halloween.* The crazies were getting cranked up and primed early.

"Nine-one-one Center," I said.

"It's my fault," he said.

"What's your fault, sir?" Another cell. I rebid the call. He's at a park in Mendon.

"This is. All of it. It's my fault."

"Where are you, sir?"

"I'm going to Hell."

You might be. "Well, where are you now, sir?" I've got a pretty solid location. His verifying it would be helpful. It's a big park. Lots of entrances. Lots of trails.

"We knew what we were doing. We knew it was wrong. At least, I did. I knew it was wrong. But that didn't stop us. It should have. But it didn't. It didn't."

"What was your fault?" I asked.

"The tests. The H7N9 testing."

I sighed, knowing I needed to control the call. Incoming ones kept stacking. "Sir, do you need police, the fire department, or an ambulance?"

I could click on a button and this guy is connected to Lifeline, where people are trained to talk with *loonies* who just needed to be heard, talked out of suicide, and sometimes just given info on how to get fed or where to find shelter for the night.

"There's no stopping it," he said.

"Stopping what?"

"Sure. You could try and blame Strong, or the U of R. It was their money. Their labs, but I could have quit. I could have walked away."

Strong? "The hospital?" I asked and cringed, upset with myself for feeding the shitstorm conversation.

"They're hungry. They'll just keep eating and eating."

I closed my eyes. "Sir, I'm going to send an officer out to talk with you. He'll just be coming by to make sure you are all right. Where are you in the park?"

"There's no point. I have a gun."

Everything changed. The call just became serious, more than checking on a caller's welfare. "Sir, why do you have a gun?"

I entered the location strictly from mapping, and put that fact on the text line. Police then know I don't have an exact, verifiable location. I add: M WITH GUN—POSS SUICIDAL. "Sir, why do you have a gun?"

"Because. I don't want to die that way."

"What way?"

"They're not dead though. They look it. But they're not. Their bodies will continue to decay, but they'll keep going, keep coming after you, keep eating until they just can't do it anymore. They get all dumb, and forget how to do things, but not how to eat. They remember that. And how to run. My God, they're fast. So, so fast."

"Who forgets things?"

"Who?" he laughed. "All of them. Everyone who got the vaccination."

"What vaccination?" I asked.

"For the flu. Aren't you listening to me?"

"Sir, I'm trying to understand what you're telling me. But I first need to know where the gun is?"

"Here. It's right here. In my hand. The barrel is under my chin."

I added that, and sent the job. "Sir, why don't you put the gun down while we talk about this?"

He laughed, again. "Are you thick, son? There is nothing to talk about. There is no cure. There is no healing them. We should have let the stupid flu run its course. Someone suggested that. I don't know who it was. They were right. But no. The government wanted the vaccination mass produced to cover up their man-made flu in the first place. With the flu and the vaccination combined—what have we done? I mean, what have we done?"

"Sir, sometimes things look bad, hopeless even, but after a good night's sleep—"

"You don't want to be around tomorrow," he said. "The lucky ones, the smart ones, will do what I'm doing—and end it."

"I don't know you, sir. But I am sure you have plenty to live for." I talked out of my ass. King Bullshit. What did I know? Maybe he had nothing to live for. "Friends, family…"

Silence.

"Sir?" I paused a beat. "Sir?"

"I just wanted to call as a way of apologizing."

"Apologizing to whom?" I asked. I didn't ask 'for what.' He thought he already told me. Too many questions in the wrong direction, and I risked angering him further. I wanted him calm, and thinking that I was helping him.

"Everyone. It won't make a difference. To me, it's at least something."

It sounded like he was wrapping up, getting ready to take action. Most suicidal callers call 9-1-1 because they aren't ready to die, and the call is an actual cry for help. This guy, he sounded different. Serious. I believed him.

"Sir, put the gun down." One of my hands went to my stomach. I winced as I sucked in a deep breath.

"You can stop them. It's futile really, but you can stop them."

He had my attention. I wanted to understand. I wanted to help. The job might be full of political shit, but helping people every night was rewarding. Gave me purpose, something I'd been running thin on since the divorce. "Stop who?"

"You have to destroy the head. The brain. It's the only way really. You take off their arms, and they'll run at you, remove their legs, and they'll use their arms to drag themselves at you. They're relentless. Fucking relentless."

This is too much. I checked the job. Police have been dispatched, but no squad cars were assigned to the job yet. I glanced at the electronic job board. It flashed in purples, yellows, and greens. There are hundreds of jobs waiting for available responders. Hundreds. Never have I seen anything like this. Never. "Sir," I said.

"The vaccinations—they were infected, a broken vile. A contaminant was released during production. No one knew. No one understood. We were under the gun. And once we did realize it. . .the government demanded a cure for the public—a prevention. We didn't have time to remake it, any of it. So we didn't stop. We just, ah God, we just kept plugging away. It was only later, you've got to believe me, it was only after that when we truly realized, really understood we'd made a huge error—that the antibody had horribly mutated. By then, what could we do? What could we do?"

I tried to put all of his nonsensical ranting into some kind of order. I couldn't. This guy was either an overworked scientist, or a nut. I'd of gone with nut at the beginning of the call. Still leaned toward nut, but . . . either way, I felt kind of sorry for him. His words made my stomach muscles tense, and ache. I couldn't seem to detach myself from his nightmare.

"Sir, what is your name?" I hoped I sounded friendly. Not like a cold call taker just doing a job.

The sound of a gunshot boomed in my headset.

I pushed back in my chair, away from the keyboards, and stared at the woods on the mapping monitor, as if I saw him. A lone man in the woods, surrounded by trees and darkness, leaning on the trunk of a Volvo or Lexus before blowing out his brains. "Sir? Sir?"

I add info: GUN SHOT. POSS D.O.A. Sent it.

I needed a break, time off the floor.

CHAPTER FIVE

"Supervisor," I yelled. Waited. Looked around. Everyone was still busy. We had over a hundred calls in Que.

I sent a message to the supervisors' pagers to look at the job. Nothing more I could do. Nothing they'd be able to do. At least I'd alerted them for when authorities called with questions.

Permission or not, it's break time. I needed a couple of minutes to get my head back together. I needed a cigarette. As far behind as we were, breaks would get skipped. I set my headset down, inactivated my terminal and walked off the floor. I wanted to look back, see how Allison was doing in the police pod, but didn't want to risk eye contact with a supervisor--didn't want to get questioned about why I was up and walking off the floor with so many calls waiting to be answered.

I patted my pocket to ensure my smokes were there, headed off the floor, through the halls, and toward the back door. The rain had stopped. The night had cleared. No need for a coat. Moon's out in a cloudless sky. Looked peacefully deceiving.

The perimeter was fenced-in. Secure within its confines. I figured I had fifteen minutes and wasn't wasting them thinking about work.

I thought about Kenya. And the scientist.

I lit my cigarette.

"They're saying they're like monsters."

I looked up. Laforce is standing there. "What?"

"On the news. The city's full of these monsters. They're attacking people. Eating them."

"Eating them? What, eating people?" I thought of the suicidal guy, what he'd said. I almost smiled. It sounded foolish. It was foolish. Best I knew, George Romero wasn't shooting a new film in Rochester.

"Yeah. It's becoming, I don't know, like an overnight epidemic."

"What, like all of Rochester?"

"I heard New York. Chicago. Pennsylvania." LaForce took my cigarette. "You mind?"

I eyed him curiously, as I lit another. "You don't smoke."

"Right now I do." LaForce took calls, dispatched both fire-EMS and police, and when needed, acted as a supervisor. He had access to more information than a schmuck like me did.

"What do you mean 'it is'?"

Laforce took a long drag. I waited. Almost counted down from five out loud. He went into an expected coughing jag. Smoke escaped from parted lips and nostrils. The big guy looked like a mildly retarded dragon.

"Give me that." I took the cigarette from him. Dropped it. Crushed the lit head with my heal.

"Guy on the news said something about scientists here at the hospital breaking some vial, and covering up the mistake. Had something to do with that flu."

"And the vaccinations."

"You already knew?"

"Just a guess," I said. I tried to swallow. Mouth was too dry. "You get one of those shots?"

"Yeah. They kind of forced everyone here to get 'em. Didn't want us getting sick and missing work, spreading it around to everyone," he said, smiled. "Why, you didn't get one?"

"Figured if everyone else got one, I wouldn't need it," I shrugged. No one can make me get a shot. I wasn't a conspiracy theorist, but I didn't trust the government much. Which, I guess, made me a conspiracy theorist.

"It's crazy on the fire side. We've sent every unit out on EMS calls. We've got fires everywhere. There's no one left. I mean, no one left. We keep putting out tones, and voicing out jobs. Inventory showed every piece of equipment at--what, forty departments-- are being used. The county has nothing left. We tried getting fill-ins from other counties. No one has anything to spare. Not a squad, not a buggy. Nothing. We're out of ambulances, too. I talked to Taylor. The police -- same thing, all out. No cars left to send to any of the newer jobs. Bunch of cops aren't answering the radio at all. So that's got cops coming off of jobs to go check on the other officers." LaForce shook his head.

It was too much to take in. I understood what LaForce said. I kept running through my conversation with that suicidal scientist. "Yeah, it's crazy on ph—"

"Grahhhhh."

I looked up at LaForce. Did he just, *Grahhhhh*, at me?

His eyes were open wide, stared over my shoulder.

I spun around.

A man had his hands on the bars of the perimeter fence. Blood dripped from his mouth, was smeared on his face, and coated his clothing. Milky, glazed over eyes vacantly stared back at us. Black veins webbed his forehead and face, pulsed. . . no, moved. I watched what looked like small pebbles being sucked up through thin straws.

"What the hell?" I backed away from the fence. "Go tell someone! Get a supervisor, or something!"

LaForce stood for a moment longer, staring. He backed away, one shuffle, then two, then finally turned and ran back into the building. I should have followed.

"It's all right, sir," I said. It's a lie. He looked sick. Like he'd died and no one had told him.

It was there. In my mind. After the call I'd just taken, after talking with LaForce. But I wouldn't say it out loud. Wouldn't even let myself form the complete thought in my head. Wasn't believing it. No fucking way zombies were real. Day of the Dead, Dawn of the Dead, Night of the Living Dead, The Walking Dead – *Fuck no*. Fuck Milla Jovovich and all of that shit.

This guy's arms snaked through the bars, fingers flicked, reaching for me. His face was pressed tight against the metal slats like he thought he could fit his head through. Worse, like he wouldn't stop shoving himself until his head *did* fit through.

I didn't see the second man until he was directly behind the guy trying to slide through the bars.

The second guy swung a baseball bat as if he was in the box at home plate. The bat connected. The first guy's skull smashed with a sickening, almost hollow-sounding *thwack!*

The face that was pressed against the bars was now halfway through. Bulbous eyes bulged from bleeding sockets. Blood oozed from a gaping mouth.

"Ah shit, man." It was all I could say. May have said it over and over. Certainly more than once. The need to turn and run back inside filled me. There was no reason to stay out here and witness a murder. There was no way I could do anything to stop it. Decided, I was ready to flee.

LaForce and Milzy stood behind me. Their mouths open. They stared at the beating taking place behind me.

"We need police," I said.

Milzy got one hand on his cell. The other reached for his waist, like he thought he wore a holster. Like his fingers were reaching for the memory of a handgun.

I couldn't look away from the --you couldn't call it a fight—scene, as the guy with the bat swung again. Blood sprayed like mist in all directions from the back of what had to be a *pulpous* mess of a skull.

Milzy yelled at the guy, "Put the bat down! Just put the bat down!"

When the assault finished, murder committed in front of us, the guy held his bat like a sword. "You have to destroy their heads, man. It's the only way. They don't go down otherwise. They just keep at you. You have to—"

Three more men came running up on the man with the bat, tackled him.

Good Samaritans?

At least, I thought that until—once they had the bat-guy on the ground—they didn't just restrain him, they devoured him.

Faces got buried in bat-guys gut, on his arm, and leg; teeth tore clothing off flesh and flesh off limbs.

One guy's head rose, intestines hung from the corners of his mouth. I wanted to look away as he gnawed and chewed and ripped the thick twisting snake of innards in half, but couldn't.

I just stood there. Thoughtless. Staring.

"Let's get inside," Milzy said. "Now!"

# # #

The 911 Office was supposed to be impenetrable. A fortress. There was a mirrored backup operations floor within the facility, and ready to go to in case the main operations area was destroyed or compromised. There were showers and rooms to rest in should a crisis present itself and we're forced to stay at work until the situation is resolved.

I figured it might happen during a major snowstorm, or some kind of terrorist attack. The idea of needing refuge from monsters on the loose never entered my mind. Never.

"I had a call, Milzy," I said. "Some guy said he was a scientist. That this was his fault. I mean, I thought he was crazy. I sent a page to you guys."

We entered the building. Milzy locked the doors.

"Saw it. Not now," he said, "save it."

"He told me the only way to stop these things was by destroying the head. Just like that guy with the bat said just now. Same thing. Destroy the head."

"Not now," he said, again.

He also told me the infected ones were people who'd received the H7N9 vaccinations, I thought.

"Get back on the phones."

The supervisor knew something. I could tell. I was shocked by what I'd just witnessed. A brutal slaying.

Milzy looked shaken. *Not* shocked.

Someone must have given information about what was going on to management. Just not to everyone, I guess. Not to us. An email. A memo. Department of Defense? The Center for Disease Control?

31

I'd been off the operations floor for maybe ten minutes?

When I walked back on, people were missing. Too many. "Where is everyone?"

"Sick. Lot of people seem to be coming down with this flu," Milzy said. "We've got them lying down in the bunker area."

"Everyone?" I asked.

LaForce had his hand over his stomach. He looked green. Normally, I'd of sworn it was from the drag he took on my cigarette. It had been a cigarette, not a cigar. He might look that way from witnessing the murder. I doubted it. He was a volunteer fireman. He'd pulled the skin off burn victims during house fires while trying to drag them out safely. No. He was not sick from smoking, and not from seeing something gruesome.

Milzy sighed. "What, LaForce?"

"I don't feel good."

"I need you on the fire side. Please. You two, get back to work." Milzy strutted back up to the center supervisor pod. Was he trying to act like everything was business as usual? Normal? That some guy didn't just get his head bashed in with a bat; and the guy with the bat eaten like he *was* a buffet?

"What the hell is going on?" I asked. I wasn't taking more calls. There were emergencies flooding the city, yes, but something really fucked up was happening here. Happening now.

Tronnes stumbled out from the fire pod. He was bent over with one hand on the chest-high cubicle wall, the other on his knee. I stepped back. Not a moment too soon. Tronnes heaved and projectile vomit spewed from his mouth and nose. It splashed onto the carpeted floor. Wet, chunky, green vomit.

He'd poised that way for ten, twenty seconds.

Looked like a fountain statue in a pond filled with slimy, but thick water. The odor of ammonia and hot dogs immediately assaulted my nostrils. My breath caught in my lungs as I jumped back and plugged my nose.

"Ah, shit," I said.

LaForce turned away. "This ain't good, man."

I kept backing up. Toward the door. I wanted out.

"Help," Tronnes said, kept reaching for me. He reminded me of the guy at the fence—the way his fingers flicked at me.

"Milzy," I called out. "Milzy!"

Milzy sat in a chair in the center supervisor chair, didn't look good. *Did he not just see Tronnes blow chunks?* Instead, his hand slipped between the buttons on his shirt, and his palm massaged his bloated-looking belly.

Spenser was on the City Fire channel. He had his headset on, but wasn't doing anything. A new job flashed on his screen. Instead of dispatching it, he stared at me. Dark bags encircled his eyes, and his upper lip kept twitching.

I knew we were out of fire equipment, there was no one to respond to anything, and I know Tronnes just got fucking sick all over the place--but Spenser should at least, at the very least, put the call out over the air.

Across the room, Allison backed away from Taylor, and Kawyn. They looked, shit . . . *they looked hungry.* "Allison!" I yelled.

She saw me, but stayed still. Her lips moved. I couldn't hear a sound she made.

I wanted to close my eyes. Ignore everything. Because it's not real. It's not happening. Couldn't be.

I could turn, run—grab my keys and head to my car. Or I could help those who were not yet sick.

But see, there's the problem.

How did I know if someone who was not sick now, wouldn't get sick? I didn't.

I tried to remember everything the scientist had said to me. He blamed the H7N9 vaccinations. They were contaminated, but still distributed to the masses. The Flu was man-made. The cure, man-made. But something had gone wrong. Locally. Only thing was the shots, the vaccinations, were sent across the U.S. Supplies may have been sent out globally? LaForce had said they were calling the outbreak an epidemic.

Epidemic was what LaForce had said.

"Who did *not* get the flu shot?" I shouted.

People looked at me from the various pods.

"Who didn't get the shot?" I said. "The vaccination. Who didn't get it?"

Maar, Nolan, Cortese—their hands went up. Like they're in school.

"What are you talking about?" DeJesus, who was on the EMS channel, stood up.

"Did you get the flu shot?" I asked.

He nodded.

I pursed my lips. "How you feel?"

"Fine." He burped.

Are you kidding me? He fucking burped.

"If you didn't get the shot, come with me."

Allison screamed. Taylor and Kawyn advanced some, moved slowly and sluggishly, but advanced regardless.

I ran her way.

Bradley-Phillips came out of the fire pod. He's a brick wall. He should have been a city fireman, not a dispatcher--doing truck work, tearing holes in roofs with saws and axes, not dispatching. When he crossed his arms over his chest and hit me, hard, I fell. I landed on my left hand. My wrist bent wrong, but didn't snap.

I screamed.

"What's the deal?" Bradley-Phillips asked.

I ignored his drooling. "You get the shot?"

"So?"

I got up, babied my left arm some, and curled it in toward my own chest. If I told them what I knew, what I thought I knew to be true, they'd panic. If I didn't come clean, those who hadn't received the shot would be trapped. I'd be trapped.

My kids. Shit. My kids!

"You're sick," I said. I moved backward a few steps. "Those of us who didn't get the shot need to go to Secondary Ops." The mirror back up area just across the hall.

I said this loud, hoped the people who had not received the shot understood. I tried to tell them without saying it. I wanted them to run.

"You don't want to spread the virus, do you, Bradley? Do you?"

He's a big guy. Normally gentle. At least I thought so before he knocked me halfway across the room.

No one moved. My subtle hint had fallen on deaf ears.

"Allison—why don't you and the others go to Secondary Ops," I said, my eyes on Bradley-Phillips, as if ready to fend off another attack. Which I wasn't. The guy could squash me with his hammerhead-sized thumb.

I couldn't leave Allison. I wouldn't say I loved her, but she was my girl. My woman. However, there was no way I planned to cross the room in order to get to her. No way at all.

I heard the groan and felt the hand on my shoulder before I could do anything. Its puke breath gave Tronnes away.

I grabbed Tronnes' wrist with my one good hand, and spun, twisting his arm up behind his back, and pushed. It was harder than I wanted to push. When I heard the crack, I shuddered.

With his now limp arm dangling at his side, I expected Tronnes to scream. Or cry. Or cuss. Or throw a punch.

He didn't. He licked his lips. Cocked his head to one side. . .And took a sloppy step toward me.

CHAPTER SIX

I'd told everyone who wasn't injected what the plan was. It was no longer safe staying here on the primary operations floor. Either they followed my directions, or they didn't.

I pushed Tronnes again, hard. His one good arm pin-wheeled.

"Allison, get out of here!"

I didn't stay to see if Tronnes fell. Instead, I turned and ran past LaForce, who was doubled over and cradling his stomach with folded arms.

I pushed through the door, pulled it closed.

Bradley-Phillips, right behind me, was stopped by the steel enforced barrier. He struggled with the door handle. If he turned it, and pushed—I'd be unable to *stop* him.

Instead, he gave up on the knob and just banged giant fists on the door's bullet proof glass.

It was in his eyes. They'd gone from brown to milky-white. Brown, to fucking milky white. Did I just see that happen? Did I just witness life spill out of his eyeballs?

No, had the scientist said they weren't dead. That they were alive? I couldn't remember.

Bradley-Phillips looked dead. It seemed like he'd forgotten how to use a door handle. In the time it took his eyes to lose color, he'd forgotten how to use a door handle. I'd seen it happen, and I still couldn't believe it.

The others—those who hadn't received the shot—made their way toward the west end primary operations exit.

Allison had jumped onto a desk and over the cubicle as Taylor swept a hapless arm toward her, and missed.

Maar, Nolan, and Cortese, were right behind her, the four of them scrambled in the direction of the only other not yet blocked possible escape route.

Winger, one of the other supervisors with Milzy, tackled Cortese, had him by the arm. Without pause, Winger bit off Cortese's ear, chewed it like a pit-bull with a rubber wad of rawhide.

I draped an arm across my stomach and hoped to steady the sudden flip-flopping going on inside there. I braced myself, an arm on the wall, knees wobbling.

I pulled my hands away from the wall. The floor blurred. My shoulder slammed into the closed door. . .off balance, but still on my feet.

Secondary Ops. It's around the corner. I pushed off the door with my shoulder, and ran.

Allison's at Secondary. Stopped at the pass-protected door. "They're in there!"

Faces were pressed against the thick, break-proof glass. Blood and saliva smeared in shapes of noses, mouths and handprints. "Milzy said the first sick people were *in* the bunker."

Didn't matter what Milzy said. Bunker. Secondary.

The sick weren't in the bunker, resting. They were in Secondary. Locked up. Locked away.

"So now what?" Nolan panted, used his sleeve to wipe sweat from his forehead. "What's going on? I mean, where do we go?"

Where do we go?

"I took a few calls—I think what's going on here, is happening out there, too," Maar said. "I have to get home. My wife and kids, you know? I have to get to them."

"It can't be safe out there," I said. I thought the same thing. My kids. I needed to find them. Protect them.

Allison looked from one operations floor to the other. They're literally twenty feet apart. Identical rooms. Both housing flesh-eating monsters that were all staring at us through blood-streaked glass, as if *we* were animals at a zoo. Or, more like *we* were food on display and they were waiting to place their order, to pick up their plate and get in line at the buffet.

Now serving number twenty-seven? I think.

"Jimmy has guns," I said, "in his locker."

I didn't want us to separate. Safety in numbers and all of that. "We can get the guns; make a dash for the parking lot. We'll follow each other. Nolan lives closest. We'll hit his house first."

Nolan smiled. He liked the plan.

"My wife's home alone," Maar said.

"I'm worried about my kids, too. We shouldn't split up," I said.

"My wife is closer," Maar said.

I just stared at him. "We're staying together. Nolan's house first. Right now, Jimmy's locker, all right?"

We ran for the men's room, through the door, past the urinals and stalls, and finally through rows of lockers. "It's this one," I pointed.

"So how do we get in?" Nolan set fists on his hips.

"Break into it," Maar said.

Way easier said than done. After ten minutes of pulling, banging, and pounding, we realized the truth. Guns might be inside that locker, but we had no way at them.

"I have to check on my family," Nolan said. He's in his locker, grabbing his cell phone, dialing. "No one's answering."

Maar disappeared. I heard another locker open.

"Come with me to the women's lockers?" Allison snaked her arm through mine. She shivered. "Please? Will you come with me to my locker?"

"I have to get to my family." Nolan put on his coat. One hand had his cell. The other, car keys. "I'm sorry. I have to."

"We should stay together." I wasn't going to beg. I didn't think anyone would listen. Not anymore.

I heard the bathroom door open. "Maar! Maar!"

Nothing. He must have taken off!

"Let's get your stuff, quick," Nolan said to Allison, and zipped up his coat.

I looked at Jimmy's locker, then at Allison, deflated. "Okay. Let's hurry!"

I got my cell, followed them out of the men's room, and into the women's. They were stopped inside.

Barb leaned against the sink counter. The faucet running. Her messy dark hair was perfect for framing a face full of clown-like smeared make-up. "I don't feel well."

"Get your stuff, Alley," I said. "What doesn't feel good, Barb?"

"My stomach."

"Go Allison. Get your stuff," I ordered. "Now."

She moved, ran to her locker.

Barb stood up straight. Like Bradley-Phillips, she drooled. Blood drop tears dripped from bloodshot eyes. Her nose twitched. Lips quivered.

When she grunts, I'm running!

"Allison!" I yelled.

"I gotta get out of here," Nolan said.

I grabbed his arm. He shrugged it off, stepped back and banged back out through the door.

Son of a bitching chickenshit!

Allison is stuck. Barb stood between us. Pupils milky-white and glazed over. *Shit.* From stomachache to zombie after seconds? That quick? That was un-fucking-fair, forget simply unbelievable!

"What do I do?" Allison asked.

Barb was all of four-foot-eleven. If that.

"Get ready, Alley," I said. I counted inside my head. One. Two...

I pivoted, raised my leg, and kicked.

The flat of my foot planted solidly across Barb's face. She fell backward, through a stall door. I saw Barb's smashed nose and missing front tooth as she landed on the toilet.

Allison didn't need to be told to run this time.

We fled the restroom and the facility and headed for the parking lot.

CHAPTER SEVEN

"Where's Nolan?" Allison asked.

I saw a car wait as the gated fence slid open. A car drove out-- *Nolan*. And zombie-monsters sauntered in. He let more of those fucking things into the *secured* parking lot!

"Run," I said.

At the parking lot, she went left. I turned right. "This way!"

"My car?"

"We'll take mine," I said. I didn't want us separated.

We get to my car. I click the fob to unlock the doors. Climbed in. Locked it.

I started the engine just as a zombie stepped in front of us. Without a second thought, I put it in second, and gave it gas. My car lunged forward and over the monster. I pulled up to the gate. Waited for it to slide open slowly, as I looked in the rear view.

Maar must have made it out, too. I was pissed he just took off, but hoped he was safe just the same.

I had the attention of the zombies roaming about inside the fence-confined parking lot.

They came our way.

Only these two were fast. Not slow and sluggish like I'd seen inside 9-1-1.

Hunger drove them.

And right now, Allison and I were the only visible meal.

The gate's mouth is open just wide enough for me to maneuver the car through. So I accelerated, smashing off the side mirror.

"Where are we going?"

"My ex-wife's. I want my kids."

She didn't ask. But we're both thinking it. My ex is just not going to hand over my kids. Thing is, I don't give a shit if Julie does or not. I'm taking them. That simple. She and the geriatric boyfriend of hers, Douglas or Donald, or whatever, won't be able to protect my kids.

"Did any of them get the shot?"

I cringed, a white-knuckle grip on the steering wheel. My ex's boyfriend is so freaking old; no way he didn't get the shot. And if he got one, then I'd bet Julie did, too.

"Your kids?" Allison is looking straight ahead.

I punched the dashboard with each word. "Fuck. Fuck. Fuck!"

I sped down streetlight lit roads. It's 10:48 PM.

People are out, filling the sidewalks and streets.

Adults. Kids.

If I didn't know better, I'd of said trick-or-treating started early.

I turned on the radio.

Static.

I checked channels.

Nothing.

I went to AM and surfed until I found a hard-to-hear broadcast, like the D.J. was holding a hand over his microphone:

> ". . . the Mexican government is allowing Americans to cross the borders. Unaffected are allowed to cross the border. There's a medical exam—if you're deemed healthy, the Mexican army is letting people cross. But they *are* shooting the heads off anyone sick. That's right. The Mexican military is shooting on-sight the obviously infected. Like I said, they are letting healthy Americans into their country. . ."

Mexico. Made sense. They were too poor a country to have received any of the vaccinations created by America. Our president put up a concrete wall to keep Mexicans out of this country. What a double-edged sword. That same wall would now benefit the Mexicans, so they could keep Americans off their soil. Funny, and almost fitting, that Mexico is getting the last laugh.

Two thousand miles away, awaits possible salvation.

I glanced at the gauges. Full tank of gas. I shut the radio off.

CHAPTER EIGHT

The expressway would be the fastest way to my ex's. For one, no traffic lights – not that I planned to stop for traffic lights. More importantly, I doubted people were walking on the expressways, not like they were walking on the other roads.

"This happened fast," Allison said. "I mean, like all at once. They like, just changed. About the only thing that tipped you off was the sickness, you know? Them getting sick."

I kept my eyes on the road. We made a left from West Main onto West Broad, and a left at the second light to the ramp that merged with I-490 W.

"Chase, Chase, this isn't happening. Not for real, right? It can't be."

"Allison, I need you to stop talking."

"Their eyes. I saw their eyes. They glazed right over. Right then, you know, right there. They just – I saw them just go from brown to cloudy, and white. I saw it. It happened. But that's my whole point—"

"Allison. Please. I'm asking. Just, I need a minute here."

"—it can't be happening. It seems like it is. It feels like it is. But it isn't, right? It can't—"

"Shut the fuck up, Allison. Please. Shut the fuck up."

She did. I felt bad. However, her voice was eating through me; frayed my nerve endings like scrapping a fork and knife on a dinner plate. "I'm sorry," I said.

"You are not the only one who's scared."

"I'm not scared."

Nevertheless, I was. I wanted my kids. I needed to protect them. I was scared for them. Not so much for me. I didn't care what happened to me. Hadn't in a while.

"We're getting out of this, Alley. We're going to snatch my kids," which was how I'd now come to think of it, "and we're outta here."

"Out of here? Rochester? And where? Where are we going? I've seen zombie movies. I have. Once you get bit, or scratched, you become one."

"That's movies. We don't know that's what's going on. Not for sure." I didn't even believe me. I still felt good saying it. That there was a chance. A way out.

"The city is infested, Chase. They're everywhere."

Not the expressways, I thought. By talking, she'd kept my mind sort of off the task of driving. I hadn't noticed the other cars, until now. These might all be people who had no idea what was happening. Maybe coming home from work, or a movie, or from out of town.

And they don't have their radio on.

No one listens to a radio anymore. Commercials suck. No. They Blue-tooth their phones, or IPods, or pay for commercial-free satellite service. They're not hearing local news. They have no idea what they were headed toward.

Or they do. And they're not headed home, but. . . west.

"Mexico."

"Mexico, what?"

"It's where we're headed."

"We're going to drive to Mexico? Why in the hell are we going there?"

She must not have heard the broadcast back when we first left the 911 parking lot. "They don't have the vaccination there. No one is sick."

"Chase, look out!"

Three people stood in our lane, headlights freezing them in place. Like deer. I punched a fist onto the steering wheel. The horn blared.

I swerved.

A car in the center lane swerved. I heard its horn.

I missed the three people standing on the expressway. Fishtailed. I pulled on and spun the wheel, trying to correct the spin, to no avail. A tire blew—a loud pop and we crossed the center and far left lane into the median, the tires biting into the wet grass like teeth into flesh.

Smoke billowed from under the hood.

Shit.

I checked the rearview mirror. I must have banged my head. The bridge of my nose and just above my right eyebrow bled. "You okay, Allison? Alley?"

She sat back in the seat, looked asleep, if not for what resembled hair coloring washed off her scalp, dripping into her eyes . . .

"Alley? Alley?" I didn't want to shake her. A small emergency medical bag was in the trunk. I climbed out of the car. Legs shook. I kept a hand on the roof, slid it along to steady myself as I made my way to the rear. If I didn't have a concussion, I'd almost guarantee Allison did.

I could not see the creatures that caused the accident. They must have ambled off somewhere. Into the woods along the right lane? It didn't matter. They were gone. For now.

I retrieved the red bag and hurried around to the passenger side. Pulled open Alley's door. Her eyes were open. She stared straight ahead.

"Allison?" Folded hands in her lap did not move. "Alley?"

I unzipped the bag. Set it on the grass.

Something burned. Close. No mistaking the grainy scents of a house fire or fires. Everything crisping at once. Not just clapboard, but furniture, clothing. Plastics and carpeting. I looked up, around. It was too dark to see much, but could imagine billowing black clouds all around me, like smoke pillars holding up the sky.

"Allison?" I tried, again, put my hands on hers. Her head turned. She faced me. Her face streaked crimson in the yellow dome light. It was blood from the cut on her head. I shuddered just the same. "It's okay. It's going to be okay."

CHAPTER NINE

I heard sirens before I saw the fast approaching police car. I squeezed Allison's hand before I let go and stood up. Starting across the grass toward the road with both arms raised, I attempted to flag the officer down. "Hey," I shouted. "Hey!"

It was R.P.D. The car slowed. The lights flashed, siren blared. Thank, God. I almost laughed. The expressway was well lit. Lampposts every so many feet on both sides of East and West bound traffic.

Things had gone out of control in the last hour. Seemed longer. Couldn't have been though. Just so much happening. The sight of a police car, responding to someone in need, that was reassuring. I felt it. Things were going to go back to normal. Whatever all of ... *this* was, it was over. Ending.

It's what I thought. It's how I felt. The smile had to show it.

But the cop? He didn't stop. He slowed. Sure. He maneuvered his vehicle close to where I was on the grass. His windows up. Blood spilled from what looked like a bite wound on his cheek. We made eye contact. I saw him see me. I know I did, before his head faced front, eyes on the road, and before his foot must have stamped down hard on the accelerator. The engine whined in protest, but surged forward regardless. Instinctively, my middle finger sprang up, the fist shot forward. I am sure I called him an asshole, too. An asshole, or shithead or something. Right now, I can't recall anything, anything other than the fact that the squad car's siren must have acted like a fucking mating call.

Two of those things came out of the woods. They weren't slow. No dragging feet, and lifeless limp arms like you see in zombie movies. Each of them looked alert. Crazed and ready to launch an attack.

I backed up a step. Another. The two approached the expressway. The shoulder.

I turned, ran for the car and as I reached the trunk, I heard brakes squealing. Something *tha-thumped*. I spun around. One of the two creatures was behind a stopped car. Not moving. Head smashed. The vehicle's front windshield shattered.

The woman driving didn't keep going. While I'd been mad at the cop for fleeing, I prayed this woman didn't do something stupid. Prayers rarely get answered.

The car door opened. She jumped out of the car. "He came out of nowhere," she said. "Out of nowhere!"

"Get back in your car," I shouted. "Lady! Get back in your car!"

She stared at me like I spoke in tongues. Like my words made no sense to her. She was so desperate to plead her case, she turned instead to the monster's companion. "He ran right in front of me," I heard her saying.

I stood there. None of this really made sense. Nothing seemed real. It all just kept unfolding. Unraveling. The second thing just ran at her. It just darted into the road, around the front of the car, and tackled her.

The *thunk* had to be her head hitting the pavement.

"Chase."

It pulled me away. Allison's voice. Thankfully, I only saw the thing lower its head, mouth open, teeth bared – and I looked away before it bit into her face. "Alley," I said, "we have to get out of here."

The tire iron was in the trunk. Best thing I could think of as a weapon. For now. I removed it. It felt heavy in my hand, solid, it should suffice. It would have to. I didn't feel like using it to change a flat tire. I didn't like the idea of being out in the open, exposed. One of the three creatures was down and out. The other feasting on the motorist. Where was the third? Still in the woods?

I did a three-sixty of the area. There were more cars just stopped, crashed, or simply abandoned on and alongside the road. Don't think I noticed it before. Not all of them. I'd been preoccupied with getting the hell away from 911. With getting Alley and myself to somewhere safe. With saving my ...

I dug a hand into my pocket. My phone. I had missed calls. A ton of texts. It had been on silent. Because of work. Even though getting to my kids was the goal, there hadn't been a second to call them. Not a fucking second.

There wasn't now. No time at all. We weren't safe here.

These things were so hungry. Just biting the shit out of people. Fucking zombies. I could hardly believe it. So much easier to refuse to believe it. The creature devouring the now dead woman proved otherwise. Proved beyond a reasonable doubt.

This shit was real. It was happening. We were in the middle of a zombie fucking apocalypse.

That professor, the guy I'd taken a call from, he'd said they'll always be hungry. That we have to destroy the brain to stop them. Destroy the brain.

Could I do that? Could I. . .

"Chase!"

I turned to face Allison. The third zombie. Don't know where it had come from. Hadn't seen it emerge from the woods like the other two. Didn't matter. It was right there. In front of me. Mere feet from Allison.

Feet.

I raised the tire iron and came at it. The thing never looked at me.

Not once. It was focused with tunnel vision. Allison was its planned dinner. When I brought down the iron, I gained the thing's attention. With a cracked skull, flattened temple – it looked up.

"Now you see me, motherfucker?" I brought the iron down again. It crumpled to its knees. The thing's hands still shot forward, fingertips brushing over Allison's pants.

She screamed. Loud. Like it burned.

I smacked the thing in the head again, and once more. The skull was in halves. The third and fourth strike was crushing through brain.

Lifeless, the body sprawled on the grass.

"We need a car. One of these other cars," I said, and smiled. An SUV was not far ahead, headlights on. Keys had to be in the ignition. "Grab the First Aid kit."

She did not move.

"Allison, I am not fucking around. Grab the First Aid kit. We're out of here." I didn't take her hand. I didn't reach for the kit. Instead, I moved around the dead zombie and ran for the SUV.

She was either coming, or she wasn't.

It was now that simple.

"Chase!" I didn't turn around. Love was important. Getting to my kids, and surviving . . . essential.

I slowed when I reached the front of the SUV. Didn't look like anyone was inside. I wasn't just going to jump in, though.

A hand on my shoulder. I should have jumped. I knew the touch. "Be careful," she said.

"Stand back," I said, and did a walk-around, checking inside the windows. Vacant. I tried the driver side door. Unlocked.

I said, "Get in."

CHAPTER TEN

The SUV cut across the median, surged back onto I-490. Thankfully, the streetlights made it seem like daytime. More and more vehicles clogged the road. Best I could guess, we'd get stuck on a shoulder not far ahead. All I could see were disabled cars. "We're gonna need to get off the expressway. Take the main roads. We don't, we're going to get—"

My cell vibrated in my pants pocket. "Stuck. We'll get stuck."

"Chase?"

"My kids, Allison." I used a knee to steer, shoved a hand into my pocket and pulled out the phone. A quick look at the screen: my daughter. "Hello? Char? Charlene?"

"Daddy?" I'd gotten both Charlene and Cash cells when their mother and I divorced; wanted direct access to my kids. Didn't need Julie acting like she had more control over my kids than she actually did. She had no clue how lucky she was, how easy I'd let her have it. Always told her if we divorced, the kids were mine. Turned out I loved my kids more than that. They didn't need courtroom custody hearings, being pulled and torn between choosing. Fuck her. *Fuck her.*

"Charlene! You okay? Where's Cash? Where's your brother?"

"Daddy, mom's sick. Something's wrong with mom. And Don too, they—they're sick, really sick. I tried calling you. I kept calling you." She was yelling. Crying. Sounded hysterical.

"Where are your Mom, and Donald? Where are you? I'm on my way there. Right now. Driving there right now. Where are they, Char?"

"Daddy? Dad?"

I looked at the phone. Still connected. "Char?"

"Watch it!" Allison reached for the steering wheel.

Instinct, I stamped the brakes, spun the wheel right, swerved around an accident scene, three cars, two bumper-to-bumper and the third t-boned. Shattered glass and a muffler covered two of three lanes. Dark . . . wetness clearly visible. Could be gas or oil. Could be anti-freeze. In all the vehicles, not one person. Not one body. Fire department wasn't coming to cut anyone out, and flush the scene. Police weren't going to issue tickets and call for a hook to clear the jam caused.

"You're right. We have to get off the expressway," Allison said.

"Charlene?" She wasn't hearing me. I couldn't hear her. I looked at the phone again. Call disconnected. I gave it to Allison. "Please, keep calling my daughter back."

Once on I-390 North, I stayed in the far right lane. Took Exit 21, Lyell Avenue. And stopped.

"Phone's dead," Allison said.

"Keep trying."

"There's no signal." She held the phone out.

"Alley, keep trying."

"Keep trying *what*? There's nothing. No signal. No bars. Nothing."

I climbed out of the SUV.

"Where are you going, Chase?" Allison's door opened. She stayed inside the vehicle. Couldn't blame her. There was no way I was getting this thing off the expressway. Ramp was completely blocked.

Charlene had been screaming for me. For her Daddy.

I needed to move cars. I absently banged the tire iron against my thigh. I walked to the front of the SUV and surveyed as much as I could see.

Get the cars out of the way was one option. I liked the SUV, wanted to keep it. But it would take too long. We'd have to cautiously check each car for keys, creatures, and bodies, move 'em, get back to the ramp, move another, and so on and so forth until a path was cleared. Then the SUV would have a shot. But for how far, for how long? Until the next roadblock. That was it. That's what we could count on. This, the mess here, it was impassable. With the SUV, in the future, maybe we could take it up onto the shoulder, across a field, through some uncertain terrain. I know it would last longer, stand up stronger to challenges than a Focus, or some small, compact hybrid piece of shit.

We'd have to find another SUV later. My kids were in trouble. I had no doubt. My fucking ex and her husband were monsters, zombies and, apparently, Julie didn't know enough not to attack and eat her fucking children.

"We have to move." I waved Allison out of the SUV. I kept looking in all directions. Too many cars left abandoned without people. Where were the people, the zombies? They had to be close. "You know what? Hold on."

I went to the rear of the SUV. "You have the First Aid kit?"

She held it up. "Right here."

I opened the back door, lifted the false floor and fished around for the SUV's tire iron. I handed it to Allison. "There ya go."

She took it, held it; eyes snaked over it like it was filled with poison. "I don't know, Chase. I'm not sure giving me this is going to make much of a difference. I don't know that I could kill a person."

"Allison, Alley, you see these things? You see anything that's happened since we left work? While we were at work, honey? Anything?" I didn't have time for this. At every turn, she was a problem. Uncertain, and wishy-washy. "Allison, take the fucking thing. And if I get into trouble, bash its head in. It's pretty simple. You love me, right? A couple. I'd do anything for you. Hope you'd do anything for me. See how this is—how it looks? So if I'm in trouble, you see one of those things on me, maybe about to bite my throat off of my neck—what are you going to do?" I pointed at her. This wasn't rhetorical. I didn't want an answer, I expected one. We were definitely at a pivotal point in our relationship. "Dear?"

"Bash its head in," she said. Barely above a whisper. But I heard it. I heard her. I could be a dick about it, have her say it again, only louder. Didn't matter. She'd said it.

"You better mean it, okay? That's all I'm saying. You better mean it. One of those zombie's gets anywhere near you, know what I'm doing? Honey, do you know what I'm going to do?" Again, I pointed at her.

"Bash its head in."

I smiled. Snapped my fingers. "Now you got it. Now you get it." I gave her a kiss, a quick hug. "We're going to figure something out. I just need my kids," I spoke softly. I knew, regardless, that I'd been a dick. "Okay? I need your help to get there, to get them. And then we're out of here."

"To Mexico?"

"Right. As of now, it's what I'm thinking."

"And we're going to be okay?"

I squeezed her hand. "We have to be strong. Right now, we've got to be like, I don't know, warriors. Can you do that?"

She nodded. "I can."

"Us. Together," I said, used the back of my hand to brush the tears off her cheeks.

"We got this. Let's get your . . . What was that?"

I'd heard it. From off the shoulder. Something climbing up the sloped embankment. Street lights lit the road. Anything off the road was shrouded in darkness. Mostly.

I saw it. Them. Faces.

"Allison, run! Run, Allison!"

CHAPTER ELEVEN

The keys were in the ignition. It was no SUV, but the Chrysler at least *looked* like it had balls. Big tires and a solid frame. It was better than walking. Except, it didn't start. Key turned; something spun and churned, but failed to connect. I need that something to kick over and the engine to rev into life.

"They're getting closer." Allison sat next to me, on her knees. She stared out windows—not just one, all of them—looking for zombies. Since ditching the SUV at the start of the expressway ramp, we'd been stuck, working to find a vehicle ahead of the disabled and abandoned cars that clogged the road leading toward Lyell Avenue.

"Think it's flooded," I said. I wanted to punch the dash. It wouldn't do a thing to help, except make me feel better.

"How long until it's not flooded."

Time was always the best way to fix such a problem. "A few more seconds before I try again."

"I don't think we've got that. They're right outside the car." Allison held her tire iron in two hands. Not like a ball player up to bat. More like a child clutching a *blankie* after a nightmare.

"How many you see?" My dad had showed me a way to beat a flooded engine. Thing was, if it didn't work, then I'd be guaranteed to have flooded it more.

"Three. No," she said, "four. I see four. All coming up behind the car."

"That it? Just four?" Four was plenty. Too many. But four was better than ten, or even five.

"It's all I see. So far. Just them, just four."

"I'm going to try something. If the car doesn't start, you slide over. You get ready to try it again," I said.

"And where will you be?"

"I'm going to get rid of those things. I don't know how this works. If they smell us, or each other. Know what I mean? All I've got is what I've seen in movies. How fucked up is that?" The call I'd taken at work, from the scientist, he'd said the things were hungry, and could only be killed for good if the head—the brain— was destroyed. I mean, that was as zombie as you get. Walking Dead shit right here.

"You're not getting out of the car," she said.

"We don't have time to argue."

"Try it," she said, "just do it."

Cars were all fuel injection. This thing shouldn't happen. Might not even be flooded. Might just be broken. I pushed the accelerator to the floor. All the way. I didn't pump the pedal. Just held it all the way down. I turned the key.

Realized I was holding my breath when nothing happened, and I exhaled. "Shit."

I reached for the door handle. I didn't think it was flooded. Didn't think it was going to start. Ever. Effectively, Allison and I were trapped.

"Where are you going?"

"This car isn't going to work." I gripped my tire iron. "Wait here."

I looked out the back windshield. Four fucking zombies. One. Two. Three. Four.

When I opened the door, I climbed out quickly, feet on loose gravel, my balance shot to shit, my right foot slid, leg extended and I went down. I didn't scream when I banged my elbow on the pavement, but I winced.

Allison screamed.

If surprise had been in our favor, maybe I'd of had the upper hand. On my ass outside the car with Allison calling out asking if I'm okay, no, nah. The element of surprise was wasted. Gone.

One of the things stumbled around toward me. It seemed slow moving. Not fast. I was trying to learn, to figure out what kind of enemy we were up against. It was like anything else. Some were fast, others slow. I'd bet some smart and some dumb as all get out. The only thing in common that I'd noticed across the board, was that they were ugly, horrendously ugly.

I took a swipe with the iron at the thing's leg. The *thunk* against bone felt hollow, and did little to slow the zombie. As it dropped to its knees, and brought its face close to mine, I tried again. Think I screamed as I swung the iron at its head. The way it had me pinned, the open car door, I had no room to angle, no way to gain momentum. I tried punching him with my weapon. It did little.

He opened his mouth. Did I see flesh wedged and flapping between the small gap in his front teeth?

It wasn't that I didn't want to die. It was that I couldn't. My kids were out there. Scared shitless. Alone. Their fucking mother was trying to eat them. I couldn't die now, not like this – not just hours into this nightmare. I've been fighting against shit all my life, more so since the divorce. I wasn't giving up here, going to die here, let this drool-faced beast eat me!

When his head shot forward, I thought it was over. Thought I was wrong, that I was going to die. When I saw the tire iron sticking out of a split skull, I let my eyes look up.

Allison breathed heavy. She'd let go of her iron, perhaps because it looked wedged in place.

That was one down, out. Three to go.

"Behind you," I said, rolling the dead thing off me.

I got to my feet told Allison to duck, and swung my iron, full swing. The lug nut end slammed like a piston into the woman's ear. The zombie cried out, shrieked. It backed up, backed away. Hands covered the ear. Blood poured, spewed from between fingers. I didn't give it time to rebound.

"I can't get mine out of his head," Allison said. She grunted. I envisioned her foot on the back of its neck as she attempted to dislodge the weapon, as if she was Arthur retrieving her Excalibur.

I swung again. The woman, already badly injured, didn't do anything except take it. In the temple. Bone shattered. Flattened. She went down. Hands no longer over her ear, but with arms straight out at her side. If that brain still pumped activity or energy through the body, I'd clunk myself in the fucking head next time.

Two down.

I spun around, expecting to have to help Allison. She chopped through the air with her iron. With a large arch that started at the spine of her back, up over her head and finished by smashing down onto the crown of the third zombie.

Stepping around *my* woman, I used the pointed end of my iron like a dagger. The man looked young. Early twenties. I saw nothing human in his facial expression. He didn't come at me. He stayed by the car behind the Chrysler. Like he'd been watching it all. As if he'd just seen three of his friends pummeled to death, but didn't have the balls to jump in and help. It was almost like if he wasn't hungry, craving a bite out of me and Allison, that he might be tempted to turn and run.

I didn't know how to handle that.

"Alley," I said.

She stood next to me. "What's it doing?"

"Nothing. Absolutely nothing."

"Kill it?"

"Let's back away. See what it does." I put my arm out. It didn't do a thing to protect Allison. The gesture made me feel better. I'd used it hundreds of times when driving. Threw my arm out in front of Charlene—even Julie when we were married—whenever I had to stop faster than normal. Of course, they'd worn seat belts. Again, it wouldn't do a thing to protect either one of them if we'd been involved in a collision. It was about the gesture.

I think.

We backed away, around the Chrysler. We were on Lyell Avenue.

The lack of people out might only be because it was so late. Still felt eerie.

"It's not coming after us," Allison said. "Why?"

"I don't know." I didn't like that answer. Did it imply more than it should? Was there still *someone* inside? Had Alley and I just murdered three people? "The others attacked. We were justified."

"We were," she said. There was no conviction in her tone. It sounded surer than when she told me she'd bash in a zombie's brains if it meant saving my life, and she had.

"Thank you," I said.

"For?"

"Saving me," I said.

"You said you'd do the same for me. Now I'm holding you to it. I do not want to get eaten by one of these things. Got me?"

We still walked slowly backward away from the lone beast. It just stood where it was, watching us.

"You kill me first. Okay? Deal?"

I nodded. I felt the same way. I did not want to get eaten by a zombie. "You think if we get bit, and don't die, we become one? Like in all the movies?"

"I don't want to find out."

I shook my head. "No. Me either."

"What now?"

I lived at one end of Greece, my kids further west at the opposite end. "We need more than tire irons. We're going to run into more of these things. Plenty more. Way everyone was pushing the vaccination shots; I don't know many people that didn't get them. I mean at work, we were like *it*."

"I know."

I didn't know much about the Avian Flu. I knew it became really popular a while back, caused a lot of deaths. I knew the government started studying each year's flu, and providing "cures" for expected strains to hit the hardest.

From what I remember, China was a player in the mess. Their government got caught messing with crops. Spreading the flu through chemicals sprayed onto farms. Crowd control at its finest. Natural Selection and all that.

"Tire irons are not going to cut it."

"What are you thinking?"

"Let's try to get to the mall." A few stores in there, the sporting goods store, and the pawnshop alone should help us stock up on useful weapons. While guns sounded good, carrying around ammo, reloading and risking gun jams didn't sound appealing. "I want a sword. Some knives. Follow me."

CHAPTER TWELVE

The mall was not close at all. From Lyell Avenue, and on foot, we had a heck of a hike ahead of us. It was dark. Things were out there. We heard them. All Allison and I were armed with were tire irons. Tire irons.

I checked my phone continually. My daughter, Charlene, had not called back. Without a signal, I was unable to call her. Naturally, my brain went wild with that. Imagining the worst possible scenarios filled my thoughts. I couldn't stop picturing my ex-wife and her husband feasting on my children. It made my stomach flip-flop, churn and grind.

Allison stuck her iron through a belt loop. The L-head held it in place. I kept mine gripped in my hand. If more of those things appeared, jumped at us from out of the shadows, I didn't want to struggle freeing the iron from the loop. Thought about sharing that tidbit of wisdom with Allison, but she looked content. Who was I to mess up her mood?

The shortest distance between two points is a straight line. I wasn't big on cutting through yards, or wandering behind buildings though. Seemed the safest route would still involve following roads, staying to the shoulder, taking advantage of as much of the shadows as possible.

We had started north down Lee. Industrial area mostly, once we walked the bridge over the canal. Homes to the right were at least a mile away to the east.

"It's so quiet now."

Allison was right. It turned out to be a good street to walk. Not sure that was what she'd implied. Still, we hadn't passed a single car on the road, which sucked. Would prefer driving. Walking took too long. If Julie and Donald were sick, and Charlene and Cash were in trouble, the longer it took me to get to their house . . . the more I worried about their safety.

"I've been thinking," she said.

"About?"

"What if we're, like it? Like the last few survivors? You said it yourself. Everyone and their mother got that shot. They gave them to people at all the corner drug stores, even. And, you saw how it was tonight at work; whoever didn't start turning into a zombie creature was getting attacked and eaten by their family and strangers." Allison stopped walking.

"We need to keep walking," I said.

"Chase, we are in some trouble here," she said.

"We need to keep walking. I need to get to my kids."

"I know that," she said. She started to walk, short, slow steps. "We're going to get them. We're going to save them from your ex. But then what? That's what I'm asking. Then what do we do?"

"We go to Mexico," I said. I tried to sound confident. She seemed to need that. "We've talked about this."

"No, I know. Mexico. But...look at our highways. The expressway looks like a parking lot. We can't just keep going from one vehicle to the next blockage, and then get in another vehicle. . ."

"Why can't we?"

"Why aren't we now? Why are we walking? You know how far the mall is? I'm already tired. My feet hurt, and I'm already thirsty," she said. "Do you see what I'm saying, Chase? The mall. We're what? Like two miles from the mall? We've come like, what? Two miles already? Know the last time I walked four miles, Chase?"

"Allison," I said.

"And we're going to what? We're going to walk from New York, from Rochester, all the way to Mexico? I'm no geography major, Chase, but I know it's like twelve hundred miles from here to Orlando. To fucking Disney, Chase. Disney. So if we were headed to Disney, Chase – guess what? We would still have eleven hundred and ninety-eight miles to go. Eleven ninety-eight." She screamed.

I grabbed her head, slapped my hand over her mouth. With gritted teeth I whispered, my lips pressed against her ear. "No screaming, Alley. I understand everything you just said. But keep your voice down."

There was no threat made. It was there. Hung between us. She had done well on the expressway ramp, saved my life, even. I'd already thanked her for that. "We good?"

She nodded; eyes open wide, staring at me. I removed my hand.

"So we're clear," she said, voice barely above a whisper, "you ever touch me like that again and I'll crack your skull."

"Good. Then we both understand what's going on here."

She nodded again. I noticed her hand on the L-head of her iron. Didn't bother me. She needed to toughen up. If she was mad at me, hated me, then fine. It would be good for her. Help her. She could thank me later.

Silence ensued. Between Ridgeway Avenue and Weiland Road, we were leaving the industrial part of the city, and entering the town of Greece. Residential areas. We could have cut down Weiland to Long Pond Road. Then north on Long Pond to the mall, but what made me say no, to continue toward Holmes Road was the thought of where Weiland hit Long Pond. Directly across the street from there was the hospital. Unity.

I had no reason to fear the hospital, but something just made me feel like with all the monsters on the street right now, the ones spilling out of the hospital would be worse. They might not be. It could be just irrational fears, but I couldn't shake it. I didn't want to go anywhere near the place. Allison didn't argue. She didn't ask why I wanted to keep on to Holmes, but she didn't argue. I was good with that.

I saw the streetlight at the intersection. I also saw more cars dead in the road. Allison had been right. It would be difficult car jumping. Taking one vehicle as far as we could, and then scrounging around for another. It could be done. Might become annoying, but that was no reason not to at least try.

"We'll check these cars up here for . . ."

"For, what?"

"Shhhh," I said. The streetlights worked shining round domes of light onto the roads, but did little to battle the darkness that surrounded us. "I hear people."

People had to be a loose term. Sounded more like animals. Grunts and groans. Moaning and yelping. What the hell were we going to do?

"Now what?" Allison had her Iron out. The belt loop had not infringed the weapon from coming free. Her other hand clutched at my forearm.

"We need to hide. See what's going on."

"Hide? Where?"

We were under the I-390 bridge. I backed us up to the stonewall. Slowly we crept forward, bent forward, staying low to the ground. It was difficult to see clearly. Ahead, I saw four, no five zombies. They looked lost, meandering about on a house's front lawn. A sixth was on the front porch.

We got closer, on the opposite side of the street, and stopped between a hedge and a parked mini-van.

"Is he knocking on the door?"

"Scratching at it, I think," I said. The guy on the porch mindlessly raked fingernails on the screen mesh. I could hear it.

I also heard a siren. It wailed, not far off. The sound brought hope. Not all was lost. Felt like it. If responders were still responding, it wasn't the end.

"What do we do?"

I didn't want to stay here, hidden on our bellies in someone's driveway. That didn't really mean we were safe. Just meant we hadn't been spotted by the small horde gathered across the way. "We can't move. Not yet. What if they see us?"

"We can't just stay here." Allison raised her head, looking left and right. "We should get closer to this house behind us. Stay low, and close, and keep moving."

"What if they hear us?"

"We run." She had a point. One that beat the hell out of mine.

Maybe I was tired too. Walking four miles had been a challenge, despite being focused, despite needing to get to my kids. Like Allison had said, I couldn't remember the last time I'd walked this far.

It was nearly midnight. I now had three things on my mind. Getting to the mall for weapons. Saving my kids from being eaten. Finding a cold beer.

CHAPTER THIRTEEN

Allison and I came up on the backside of the mall. From where we crouched in the bushes, we could see the loading dock side of Target. Beyond that, Sears and Penny's. The sporting goods store sandwiched between them. The mall had front entrances to all the stores. The back also had direct store entrances, as well.

The lot had parked cars, which was good. We'd need them. They provided cover. The roaming mass of zombies looked a bit overwhelming.

"There's a lot of them." Allison knelt beside me, one hand on my shoulder. "Look at 'em all."

"I can't shake how it's just like every stupid zombie movie I'd ever seen. They're just, just roaming around. Like they are hungry for brains."

"Don't say that," she said.

I didn't need to say it. We'd seen it. Watched as people we worked with, attacked other employees. We'd barely escaped work. A hard fought walk to the mall. These things, although maybe not craving brains, did seem interested in biting non-infected people to death. Bad enough in my book.

"We need to get to the mall. Can't imagine the doors are locked," I said. I looked around the lit lot. There was no visible clear path. If we did a serpentine between vehicles, we stood a chance.

"Bound to be more inside the mall, too." Allison merely pointed out the obvious.

"We get in, and weapons are all to the left."

"Just got to get across the parking lot."

"It's what I'm thinking."

I watched what could be a group of four meander toward a Lexus. Couldn't be more than a hundred, maybe a hundred and fifty yards to the left. They didn't appear distracted, however, they all seemed to lumber forward in the same general direction. That direction was away from us.

On the right, zombies weren't as congested, but scattered. It was the same kind of slow and sluggish . . . gait. I counted ten, no . . . eleven. Twelve. Yes. I saw twelve.

"Look at him." I followed Allison's finger. Straight ahead. Just past a light pole. A guy ran toward us. He was a ways out, but running in our general direction. "Sick?"

"Looks it," I said. The guy's arms flailed, pin wheeled. He looked like someone trapped in the midst of a swarm of bees. "What   is   going--"

He wasn't sick. Not a zombie. This became obvious as he screamed for help. Although my exposure to the infected was limited, I had not heard a single one of the creatures talk. They moaned. They grunted. They bit. They ate. That I'd witnessed. Talking, not so much.

"Help! Please! Please, God, help me!"

I didn't know where he thought help might come from. I did know his screaming sure as shit attracted the unwanted attention. The creatures that had reached the Lexus turned, almost as one, and faced the running man. The expensive sedan forgotten, they moved -- a bit quicker, as if with more purpose -- toward the screamer. The other twelve also seemed to zero in on the man.

"What do we do?" Allison had a hand on her iron.

"What do you mean?"

"How do we help him?"

This time I planted my hand on her shoulder. "We're going to the sporting goods store. He's created a perfect diversion for us."

Allison stared at me, eyebrows furrowed. "Chase, he's a person. Not a diversion."

"He's an asshole. Why the hell was he screaming, why was he running--?"

Then I saw it. *Them.* No other way to classify it other than a herd. Not like cattle. Maybe a pack was a better description. Like wolves. Another fifteen, I don't know, could have been as many as twenty zombies, rounded the corner by the Sears building. *Rounded* that corner like a New York Yankee rounding first, sprinting for second.

"Are you shitting me?" I said out loud. "This asshole's going to get all three of us killed. He's running right for us."

And closing the distance fast.

"Okay. Okay," Allison stumbled. "So now what do we do? Where do we go? We need to hide."

I didn't remind her that a mere second ago she was trying to get me to help the madman. Didn't blame her. Maybe we could have saved him from a handful. The zombies in the parking lot had been slow movers. Everything changed with the new . . . pack added to the equation.

Hated to admit it, but part of me hoped the guy was taken down. It was a heartless thought, possibly a chicken shit thought, but there it was, swimming around in my brain. I needed to get to my kids. I needed weapons. I didn't know this guy. He meant nothing to me. It was not much different from the training I'd received at work. One call at a time. Enter the job and don't look back. Go on to the next call.

"Chase?"

I opened my mouth, about to suggest a solution, when they got him. One zombie from the pack leaped forward. It was a great tackle. Arms wrapped the running man's waist, and legs, while its shoulder drove into the back, and down the two went.

The group was on them instantaneously. A genuine dog pile.

"We have to go," I said. "Diversion or not, this is our chance."

Allison stared at the unfolding feast. Eyes wide. She didn't respond, but followed behind me. We stayed low and ran as fast, and as quietly, as we could. We skirted the parking lot, staying out of the spray of lights.

I kept one eye on the massacre. Aside from the fast zombies, the slow moving ones were closing in. Couldn't imagine there would be much meat left for sharing.

God, did I just think that?

What was wrong with me? There wasn't much meat left. I shook my head. I needed to stop. Allison was right. That had been a man, someone probably with a family. I had wanted to use his . . . screaming, as a chance for us to escape. That was terrible enough. I didn't need to think of him as mere meat, too.

We made it to a caravan. We slammed our backs up to the side panel. We were out of view, could no longer see the man being devoured. Ripped apart. Hopefully, they not only could not see us, but had not noticed us, either.

"I was going to let him die," I said.

"What?"

"I don't know what's wrong with me. That man, I had no intention of helping him. None."

Allison took my hand, gave it a squeeze. "We need to get into the store."

She was right. Nothing I could do now. Maybe nothing could have been done, regardless. Still, I was pissed. Mad at myself. This was not me, not who I was. Not who I wanted to be.

Weapons.

The sporting goods store.

"Okay. Let's get inside." I stuck my head around the front of the van. Most of the zombies were staggering about in the general area. I closed my eyes at the sight of the fallen man. He'd be torn apart. Literally. Chunks of remaining limbs and pieces of discarded flesh littered and displayed in three spots in that section of the parking lot.

The pack of zombies stayed together. They were the ones that made me most apprehensive. They weren't headed towards us, but they were headed back towards the mall.

"It's now or never, Alley. You ready?" I asked.

"I guess," she said.

I looked at her, and almost yelled. A zombie had snuck up on us.

It grabbed Allison's hair and yanked her back and off her feet. .

CHAPTER FOURTEEN

The zombie needed to reset his stance after dropping Allison to the pavement, before falling to his knees over her.

Allison let out a scream. Her hands clawed at his face, and her feet kicked out at nothing. She tried rolling onto her back in an attempt to scramble away.

I struggled getting my tire iron out of my belt loop. It was wedged. Panicked, I gave up on the lodged weapon, and reeled back with my leg and face-punted a solid kick to the side of the zombie's head.

My boot knocked the thing sideways, but not off Allison entirely. Its hands held fast to her hair and shoulder. I kicked again, this time, standing over it, clobbering the heel of my boot on its temple.

The drive pushed him down and off my girlfriend. I jumped up, and stomped down on his skull, and again and a third time. The fucker's hands still reached out for Allison. She was up, and out of reach.

"Chase," she said.

"I got him," I said. I managed to get the iron free. I raised it over my head and smacked it down onto his forehead. The brow split. Blood sprayed.

Allison tugged on my shirt. "Chase. They heard. They're coming."

I didn't need to look around to understand. I knew what she meant. I knew we were now in trouble. "We need to get inside."

We ran.

The slow zombies marched our way. I saw that. The fast ones, the pack of quick zombies, they had us in their cross hairs as well. Timing was essential and obvious. We needed to reach the doors to the store before the zombies reached us. It would be close, photo-finish-close.

My legs pumped as hard as they could. All I kept thinking was, don't trip, don't trip, don't trip. I saw it in my mind though, tripping over my feet, falling to the ground, and being eaten by monsters that--by all intent and purposes--shouldn't even be hungry anymore. *Gluttons.*

Allison ran alongside me. I heard three things. Us breathing, their feet pounding pavement--and that pounding of pavement getting louder and louder.

Safety loomed yards ahead. Just yards. The way I bounced as I ran made the sliding doors seem to shake. It's how my brain felt. Jumbled and loose, sloshing freely around inside my skull.

Then I heard, above our breathing and shoes pounding pavement, the groans. The moans. So loud, so angry. They sounded like a chorus of cries, like hundreds of fingernails raking across a chalkboard.

We were almost to the doors, to the sanctuary of the mall, but so were they.

I held my tire iron raised in the air as I ran. If any of those things got in the way, tried blocking those doors, I'd be ready.

Thirty feet from the door, it looked like we'd make it. Once inside the store we could quickly scramble for more useful weapons.

Or could we?

The doors were automated. If we entered easily, so would they.

And then it didn't matter. As we reached the doors, as the doors slid open, one of the zombies reached us. Blocked our entrance.

Allison stabbed the pointed end of her iron into the thing's face. Through an eye-socket. I heard a pop. Saw juices fly. She didn't even try to pull her tire iron free. She left it, jumping over the falling body and through the open doorway. I was right behind her.

The bad thing? The zombies were right behind us.

Inside the store, Allison went left, to where I'd said weapons would be located. I followed, hoping they'd be accessible. We wouldn't have time to pick through items searching for what might work best.

"Grab something," I said. "Anything."

Anything. There was nothing. Hunter camo, deer stands, rain slickers, shoes. Where were . . . what? If guns were on display, they wouldn't be loaded. Bows would be behind counters. I expected to raid the store, as if shopping without paying. I didn't think we'd be chased into the store.

"Allison, get to the mall, run for the mall!" I shouted, as I changed direction. Down an aisle, I saw the mall.

"Guns," I heard. She was behind me. I didn't think she was following me. I didn't want to look back. I didn't need to see the zombies closing in on me. Didn't want to see them trapping her in the corner section of the store where weapons were kept.

The boom echoed.

I chanced a look back, just as another shot was fired.

Shit. Only one of the zombies followed me.

The rest were on her ass. She'd never make it. She *did* have a gun.

A third shot resounded.

I stopped fast, snatched a composite hockey stick from the rack, and spun around. The slap shot was a wide arc cutting up through air and slicing the side of the zombie's neck. The cut wasn't deep, but the artery severed. Blood jetted from the wound as I pulled back on the stick and swung at its throat a second time for good measure. The thing dropped to its knees, and face planted onto the tiled floor. I stepped over the beast as blood pooled around its head.

"Allison!" I started toward the back of the store. Two more shots were fired. At least I knew she was alive.

"Chase!"

Alive and calling for me. I ran as if on ice, the hockey stick in both hands. Only thing missing, the pads. I'd of loved to have been decked out in some hockey gear.Zombies' would have a hell of a time gnawing on my flesh through all of that gear!

Allison ran out into the main aisle. It almost got her slashed with my stick. It also almost got me shot. The handgun was aimed at my face. I ducked, and swatted the space between us, as if I could bat a bullet out of the way like a fly, had she pulled the trigger.

"I killed like five," she said. Her arm fell to her side. The threat averted.

"No time to brag," I said. They followed her. Fast. "This way."

We ran back the way I'd just come. The body of the bloodless zombie sprawled out on the floor was a small hurdle. Jumping over him was not the issue. It was the sticky blood around its head that became the problem.

Allison slid. A red smear trailed two feet out of the puddle. I clutched her arm as she fell backwards. It did nothing to stop the fall. She cried out as her shoulder popped from the socket.

"Give me the gun," I said.

She wasn't listening. I wretched it free from her limp arm, knelt beside her and nothing. Empty. I dropped the gun, scooped an arm under Allison and lifted her to her feet. "Run," I said, needlessly.

Staying back, I swung the hockey stick at the next closest zombie. I was not lucky enough to slice an artery, but the stick did the job and smacked hard enough into the creature's head to knock him off his feet. He went down hard. Sprawled out on the linoleum for the count. I straddled its body, raised the stick like an ax, and swung at his skull over and over as if splitting firewood.

"Chase!"

I almost couldn't stop. Didn't want to stop. My adrenaline was surging through my body like crazy. I could feel it pumping through every limb. I hacked at the smashed head one last time, and the blade on the hockey stick lodged into the gash. I needed to step on its shoulders and pull with both hands to free my new weapon of choice.

Then I ran.

CHAPTER FIFTEEN

Greece Ridge Mall turned out not to be the sanctuary I'd hoped. Allison and I were now inside a mall with zombies, and no closer to saving my kids than we had been when on the road. There was no more time to kill. I needed to figure out how to get to my ex's house, fast.

"We need to get out of here," Allison said.

There had been a zombie movie I'd seen. People gathered and took refuge inside a mall. Maybe that had been part of the reason I'd thought to come this way. The weapons in the sporting goods store influenced the decision, sure. The difference had been that the zombies were outside the mall. Not shoppers and employees and . . .

"Mall security," I said. "We need to get to the food court."

"Security isn't going to be able to help us," she said.

We squatted by the Piercing Pagoda Kiosk. Right now, I didn't see a single zombie in the mall's aisles. Maybe they were all inside the various stores. Maybe the few we'd led into the sporting goods store were it. Wherever they were, I was thankful for the reprieve. I worked on calming my breathing, settling my nerves. "I don't want security's help. I want their guns. The keys to their vehicles."

Arming mall security guards came not long after the town curfew. Teens under 18 were not allowed to be in the mall without an adult. It was meant to keep riff-raff to a minimum. Worked for a while. The gangs of teens had people 18 years old with them, and so by the mall's own rules, could stay. And wreak havoc. And did in fact, wreak havoc. For some time, Greece Police kept a presence as well. Eventually, they needed to pull back. The town was too large to tie up officers patrolling the inside of a mall.

"But the roads. You saw how bad they were. We won't get a mile in one of those pick-up trucks," she said.

"Even a mile, driving, is better than a mile walking. Safer."

She pursed her lips, nodded. She agreed. "Okay. The food court."

When I had been a kid, this mall used to be two separate malls. A transformation took place in 1994. The two were joined. The extension that connected them was filled with additional stores, and at the center -- a huge food court was added. In total, the place took up over 1.6 million square feet. We were at one end of the mall. Had to go halfway, since the security office was located in the food court.

I lifted my head and peered around spinning displays of gold earrings and necklaces. I still did not see a single zombie around. "If we stay close to the center of the aisle, we have plenty of plants, and garbage receptacles and kiosks to hide behind. Looks like nothings out here, but we're gonna move like the military, okay? I go, I check the area, and then you go -- moving past me to the next spot to hide behind. You check the area, then I'll pass you and move on to the next spot. See what I'm saying?"

She nodded. "I get it. Like S.W.A.T."

"Exactly. Like S.W.A.T."

She had no weapon at all. I had the blood and brained hockey stick. I should give it to her. Would she be able to swing it hard enough to kill a zombie? Truth is, if I kept it, I'd have a better chance of saving her and me, should another attack occur. That was just a fact. Or was it that I just trusted myself more than I trusted her? No matter. I was keeping it. Decided.

I took out my cell phone. No new calls. I sent a fast text to my daughter: Daddy's coming. Stay where you are!

"Anything?" Allison asked.

I just looked at her. "You ready?"

She let out a breath of air that made her hair blow. "As I'll ever be."

"I'll go first. You see anything, don't yell. Okay? No yelling."

She frowned, clearly not happy with so much instruction. I wish she understood, while I hoped to get us safely from point A to point B, my kids were the priority. She had to concede to doing things my way. No questions asked, or I'd leave her ass behind. It was that simple. I didn't want to have to say it though. I just needed her to know it.

"On three?" she said.

"What?"

"You going on three?"

I closed my eyes for one long second, avoided shaking my head. "On three."

"One, two," she said, and then silently mouthed, "three."

I stayed hunkered forward and ran around and past a Pagoda, and stopped at the table and three 7-foot poster stands that promoted the fitness center near the movie theater at the extreme opposite end of the mall. The posters provided excellent cover. I could stand and be hidden. I didn't. I stayed low. I did a 360 and made sure nothing saw my short sprint. Didn't seem like anything had. My heart was racing once again. The calming I'd done earlier, forgotten. The blood was pumping fast. My cheeks felt hot.

Inside Burlington, I saw two zombies. They wandered aimlessly amidst racks of marked down clothing. They looked hapless, and bored, resembling live shoppers as far as I was concerned. They seemed preoccupied with absolutely nothing. I had not attracted their attention.

The last thing I needed was for them to see Allison when she ran. I spun around, looking toward the Sprint store, and Abbotts Ice Cream. The west aisle was clearer, best I could tell.

I tried to use my hands to explain I wanted Allison to run on the opposite side of the Pagoda--not taking the same path I'd used. I snaked my hand toward the right, and waved her on.

I saw it in her eyes. She had no idea what I was trying to communicate. None. I gave her some credit. What I did with my hand resembled bad charades. I kept at it. I used two hands to wave her in on my left side, and then shook my head, NO. On the right side of my body, I did it again with my hands, and nodded vigorously, YES.

She nodded. Thank God. She moved to the other side of the Pagoda, and then found me with her eyes. I looked all around, thought it was safe, and nodded with a simple wave of my hand.

Staying low, she ran toward me, and was about to kneel next to me.

The plan forgotten.

"Keep going, to the next area," I whispered. "Go, go."

Allison looked toward Burlington. I know she saw the zombies inside, because her eyes opened wider.

"Go," I said. "Stop behind the next kiosk."

She ran. I watched. I tried to see everything at once. When Allison stopped, sat, rested her back against the wristwatch kiosk, I inhaled deeply, and sighed silently. When she waved me to her, I shook my head. She had not scanned the area for zombies at all.

This was not going to be simple.

CHAPTER SIXTEEN

Somehow we'd managed to leapfrog our way from the Pagoda kiosk to a center aisle kiosk that sold electric cigarette kits. This time, instead of running past Allison, I stopped and dropped beside her.

We both were breathing heavy. Sweat rolled down her forehead. She wiped it from her brow with a forearm. "I'm not sure how much more I can do," she said.

"We're there. Security is just around the corner. Once we get into their office, we're bound to find weapons. At least keys to one of their patrol vehicles." I knelt, ready to make a break for it.

"It's not what I mean," she said. "I'm not sure how much more of this I can do. Running. Hiding."

I shook my head. "So what? You're going to give up? Just sit here and wait for one of those things—or a group of them—to find you? You saw them take down that guy in the parking lot, the people at work. You don't have much of a choice. We're going to arm ourselves and get out of here."

She almost laughed, the smile faltered. "And get your kids and go to Mexico. Mexico. Chase, do you realize how crazy that sounds? How impossible?"

I heard moaning. Groaning. We were not alone. Not like we had been for most of our excursion from one end of the mall to its center. Made sense the food court might be more dangerous. The smells. Probably drew them from all corners, like flies to shit.

"The alternative is giving up, Alley. Surrendering. I'm not going to do that. I can't. You can't either."

"Because of your kids. I understand that. You have to keep going, keep moving. But not me," she said.

"I'm not leaving you here. You'll die. It'll be a horrible death, Alley. Painful. If we end up going that way, then we go that way. You aren't giving up this easy. Not now. Not while we have options. I won't let you," I said.

I watched her lip tremble. Tears pooled in her eyes. "When I say run, we're running. Together. I'm not leaving you here. Got it?"

She nodded. "Okay."

Had she disagreed, giving me any more problems, I would have left her. She just didn't realize it. If she couldn't toughen up, she was going to find herself on her own. She might think she's tired, ready to quit. Once death faced her, I bet she'd run in the opposite direction screaming. No one gave in, gave up that easily when actually in front of death. No one. It went against natural instinct to survive.

"On three," I said, smiling. "We got this, okay?"

"On three." She knelt beside me.

I held a hand up, scanned as much of the mall as I could see. "I don't see anything."

"I hear them."

I nodded. "I have a feeling when we round that corner; they're going to be there."

"So the plan?"

"We run past the Burger King, toward the restrooms, and here's the thing – we try the security office door. If it's unlocked, we can get in; lock ourselves inside if we're chased."

"Is that a good idea? Locking ourselves in there?"

"That's if we're being chased, and it's unlocked. Otherwise, we get in, grab what we can. Flashlights, radios, weapons, and keys. That's the main thing, keys."

"And if it's locked and we're being chased?"

"Fire exit doors are right there. We just go out and keep running until we're not being chased anymore. Got it?"

"On three," she said, again.

"Yes. On three." We counted together.

On three, we stood and ran.

We passed the Cookie Place, and Burger King, ran down the short hallway that led to both the restrooms on the right and stopped at the security door across from them. We did not need to turn to see that zombies ensued. Lots of them. Thankfully, slow runners. About the only break we've had so far.

I grabbed the knob and twisted. The door opened. Second break. We entered the postage-stamp sized office and closed the door, and squatted down. The room was mostly windows. If the things didn't see us enter, they didn't need to know where we were. From the floor, I scanned the room. A radio charging base was on the counter. Three of the five radios were missing. Two were left, and hopefully, were fully charged.

"Flashlight," Allison said.

I followed her line of sight. It was long, looked solid, like it might be filled with six D batteries. It could serve two purposes. Light, and as a weapon.

Staying low, I tugged on cabinet drawers. They were all locked. I didn't see guns anywhere. Which made sense. Now. The guards probably had to supply their own weapons. The mall wasn't going to stockpile an armory. I shook my head, discouraged.

"Help me find keys."

"What kind?"

"Keys. Any kind," I said. "You take the flashlight."

She carefully reached up and took it off the counter. "It's heavy."

"You can use it to bash a zombie's skull, okay?"

She nodded. "The radios?"

"We're taking those, too. But right now, keys."

Checking anywhere that wasn't locked inside a drawer, we came up empty. No keys. That was a strike. I really wanted a vehicle. I had to kneel to reach the radio charger. As I removed the two radios, I chanced a look at the windows and almost vomited.

They'd been quiet. Maybe just watching us. Like they were at a zoo, and we were animals in a display. At least ten zombies, hands and faces pressed against the glass. Bile and blood and filth scummed up the windows.

"Okay," I said, sitting on the floor next to Allison, our backs pressed against the door. "We're kinda screwed."

"Why? What?" She said. "They're all out there, aren't they?"

I nodded.

"A lot?"

"A lot."

Allison turned on one of the radios. It squawked. Chirped. Then static hissed through the tiny speaker. She depressed the button on the side. "Hello, anyone? Hello?"

When she released the button, more static. She spun the top knob, switching channels and repeated her greeting.

"Maybe they're short wave. Reach out only a mile or so?" I said.

"What do we do, I mean, how are we going to get out of this room. It feels like a coffin now."

It did feel like a coffin. I felt claustrophobic. Tried to control my breathing. Unless these things got bored, we were literally trapped. Stuck in place. Making a run for it would never work. There were too many. And they held the advantage being on the opposite side of the door.

A loud bang sound. Not like a gunshot, but as if something crashed, fell over. I snuck a peak, kneeling. "Well, that got their attention," I said, sliding back beside Allison.

"What's that mean?"

"The things, they all looked to see what the commotion was, too. Some even wandered toward the sound."

Alley smiled. "They did?"

"Don't get all happy. A few left. The rest--they're still right outside this office."

"Nah. I got an idea. Watch this." Allison crawled toward the counter, reached up and came back with a microphone on a stand. She held down the button on the base, and started shouting. Her voice echoed throughout speakers hung in the mall. "Anything?"

I looked at the window. "You've got their attention. Thing is, there's a speaker right outside here. Think there's a way to isolate what part of the mall gets the transmission?"

"The switchboard?"

I went to where she had retrieved the microphone. The small switchboard had levers that were labeled. There were stores, and sections--north, south, west, and east. This might work, I realized. J.C. Penny was the biggest store, opposite the food court. I toggled the switch, and nodded at Allison.

When she yelled, it was too loud. The creatures outside the security office banged on the glass, and walls. "A little softer," I said. The things weren't going to investigate noise far away, when she made enough noise to hold their interest right here.

Allison turned her back, hovered over the microphone, and tried again. It was perfect. While I heard her voice out in the mall, I barely heard her, and I sat right next to her. I looked at the switchboard, and found the volume knob. I turned it up. "Keep going," I said.

I turned to look at our visitors. Most were gone. Not all. But most. I tried not to make any eye contact. I felt like that might engage them. I don't know if that mattered, or if they just smelled our life. I wanted to do as little as possible to have them attracted to us. Right now, avoiding eye contact was about all I could think to stop.

"They leaving?" Allison said.

"Yeah. Don't stop." I closed my eyes. Kept them shut and didn't move at all. I tried to control my breathing, taking slow shallow breaths. Inside my head, I counted to sixty. When I opened my eyes, they were gone. The remaining few zombies had left. "I think we're clear. Don't stop. Not yet."

I chanced a look. The last of the zombies left the area, entering the food court, a compound fracture at the ankle left the foot dragging behind with each pull of its leg.

We had the two radios, the flashlight, my hockey stick, but no keys. No guns. It was not what I had hoped for, but it was what it was. We'd have to make the best of it. Staying inside the security office was the worst thing we could do. The mall was clearly not a safe haven. Running outside the emergency exits might not prove any better, or safer. And yet, that was our only choice. Making a run for it.

"We're going to do this. As soon as you stop transmitting, we're going to bolt for the exit and just keep running. Okay?"

She nodded, but never stopped talking into the microphone.

I gave her a three count. I knew she liked them, and then she stood. I stood, and pulled open the office door. I tried to be quiet about it. We didn't seem to gain any attention. We rounded the office. The emergency exit was a mere twenty feet away. Just had to run past the restrooms.

I ran, hit the bar across the door and pushed it open. Lights flashed. Sirens blared, and above it all, I heard Allison scream.

CHAPTER SEVENTEEN

I stood at the threshold. One foot out of the mall, one inside. The cool night air was a blast of refreshment after working up a sweat traipsing through the mall like S.W.A.T. and then being trapped inside the tiny security office for the last hour.

One of the things had come out of the bathroom. It had Allison by the arm. She struggled against its hold. Squirming, and wriggling her body trying to pull free.

This one was a mess. Over three hundred pounds, it appeared he must have turned while on the toilet. His khaki trousers were down around his ankles. Decaying white legs were mixed with hair, throbbing veins, and puss oozing from open wounds around his thighs. His Canary yellow dress shirt was buttoned as if a blind man had assisted. The mismatch of buttons to holes made the front tails lopsided around a pair of whitey-tighties that looked so tight they had to be cutting of blood supply to the creature's brain -- if blood still flowed through its bulbous body.

"Allison!"

She stopped struggling. Must have realized what I was about to say. Before I could yell, she swung a backhand. The handle of the flashlight cracked square against the bridge of the zombie's nose. Perhaps it was the pants tangled around its feet, but stumbling back a step, the fat monster lost his balance and went down, backward. Hard. Its head smashed into tile. Blood sprayed from underneath.

It hadn't let go of Allison, pulling her down as well. She was able to wretch her harm free. Back on her feet, she delivered a kick into the fallen zombie's exposed gut. Then another. And despite the other zombies now drawn to the excitement down the corridor, and our window for escape narrowing, she dropped to her knees by its head and beat its skull with the butt of her flashlight until blood coated the metal and it slipped from her hands. Crying, one forearm pressed to her face, Allison picked up her weapon and pushed off the ground to stand back up.

"Allison, we need to go." I held out my hand.

She looked down at the man she'd killed. Only it wasn't a man. Not at all.

"Allison," I said.

Blood smeared tears stained her cheeks. She huffed, gaining control, and walked toward me. It was a big moment for her, a life altering one. The converging zombies were close, getting closer. "We need to . . . run. Now."

She chanced a look back, saw what I saw, and snapped out of whatever mode she was stuck in. She ran. I pushed open the door, and we were outside in a heartbeat.

Headlights shined in our eyes. The sound of a motor running. We stopped as the door closed behind us. There was nothing to block it with. The zombies could exit the mall as easily as we did.

"Who's in the truck?" I yelled. "We just want to get somewhere safe!"

No one answered.

Allison and I circled around the vehicle. She went toward the passenger side. I went around to the driver's. No one was inside the pickup truck.

"Get in," I said just as the emergency door opened and out came a flock of slow moving zombies. "Get in, Allison!"

"It's locked," she shouted, as I opened the driver-side door. I looked around for the button to unlock the doors, checking the inside panel. I couldn't find any.

"Chase!"

I leaned across the seat, grabbed the handle and pushed open the passenger door. Allison scrambled in, slamming the door closed before any of the zombies reached her. "Too close," she said.

I sat up, set my foot on the break, and shifted it into reverse.

"You should plow right into them," Allison suggested.

Instead, I checked the mirror, looked behind me and backed up. There wasn't time to run over zombies that weren't able to harm us. This wasn't a search and destroy mission. The goal was getting to my kids. Same as it has been all night.

I spun the wheel and floored it, heading toward the exit onto West Ridge Road; thankfully the parking lot was mostly empty. I only needed to swerve around a Prius and a Beamer. The rest of the road was clear.

The streetlights were on, flashing reds and yellows. Power issues, no doubt. There would be no one to fix them. They would stay that way until the city lost juice and Rochester was drowned in darkness. My guess, it wouldn't be long. Not with no one manning the utility companies.

That thought forced me to realize the apocalypse in full. No electricity. Water and food supplies would be an issue. Maybe. There had been so few . . . survivors that Allison and I had encountered so far, that grocery stores would be ours for the taking. Possibly. Hopefully.

At the intersection, I made a right heading eastbound on West Ridge Road in the westbound lane where less disabled cars cluttered the street.

Still had to swerve back and forth, and onto the median at times, but for the most part, we were moving, and making good time. Finally.

At the flashing lights, I turned left onto Stone Road. I lived in the apartment complex on the right, but decided against stopping home. I didn't want to waste any more time. Too much had already lapsed. I needed to get to my kids. Last time I'd checked my phone, there was nothing from my daughter. That made me more than apprehensive.

Allison silently looked at me as we flew past the complex. She must have known what I was thinking, too. As we came upon the Ridge Road Fire Department, two men ran into the middle of the street. Both waved an arm and a baseball bat in the air, as if they thought we were going to stop.

I dropped my foot on the accelerator.

"What are you doing?" Allison screamed.

"They have weapons!"

"We have weapons."

They jumped to the left and the right out of the street as I blew past them.

"Chase, they're human. They need help."

I wanted to argue. Instead, I thought of the man in the mall parking lot. He died so we could raid the stores. Despite coming up empty handed for the most part, he'd been eaten for us. I remember how that made me feel.

My feet punched the brake. Tires squealed. Couldn't see it in the darkness, but knew black rubber was laid down over the pavement. Could smell the burn.

I checked the rear-view mirror.

Both men ran at the security truck. I'd have left them had I assumed it was aggressive. The horde of fast zombies behind them, gaining on them, told me otherwise. I laid on the horn. The sound blared like a goose in heat.

They didn't need the warning. They seemed to realize they were being pursued. They, together, reached the rear of the truck and jumped over the tailgate. I didn't wait to make sure they were all set, before flooring it. More squealing. More rubber laid down. And we were out of there.

Allison looked over her shoulder, slid the small window between us open. "You all right?"

"Oh my, God, thank you. Thank you for stopping."

"You almost killed us. What the fuck were you --"

Allison closed the window.

"Not very appreciative," I said.

"But alive," she said.

We rounded the corner. Mt. Read Boulevard was the next intersection. Cars were backed up. Lights on. If I didn't know better, I'd have sworn people were inside them just waiting for the light to turn green.

The flashing red made it clear. No one was waiting. And people were not going to be inside those abandoned vehicles. I was not about to give up the truck. It was one of the best things to come from attempting to raid the mall. I drove up over the curb. Our passengers bounced around in the back of the cab. Even with the window between us closed, I heard cussing. I went onto grass and straddled the sidewalk.

There was no stopping us now. Seemed like only a few more blocks and we'd be at my ex's house. It was more like a couple of miles. They lived in Charlotte. Big house by the lake. Once we got there, though, I'd have my kids. Safe, and sound and with me. Then we would be able to plot our plan out of the country.

Part of me allowed a sense of goodness, and hopefulness, and a bit excitement to sink in. Until a loud bang shattered the euphoric feeling.

I gripped the wheel, but because of how fast I was driving, lost control of the truck right as we reached Mt. Read.

The crash sent my head forward. It slammed against the steering wheel. And darkness swallowed me whole.

CHAPTER EIGHTEEN

"We're not mall security, or cops."

It was Allison talking. My eyelids fluttered open. Closed. Then parted slightly.

A dark face outlined in a halo of streetlight loomed in front of me. Over me, I realized. I was lying down. The grass felt wet. The ground hard, and cold. I smelled smoke. Gasoline.

"Chase?"

"Everyone okay?" I said.

"You drive like an asshole," a man said.

"Everyone, but you." Allison held my hand.

"I need to sit up." I pushed up onto an elbow, shook my head slowly. My vision blurred. I closed my eyes.

"You okay?"

"Yeah. I will be."

"You still drive like an asshole," the man said.

"This is Josh," Allison said, "and his brother Dave."

"Thanks for stopping for us." It was Dave. He held out his hand. I didn't reach to shake it. Feared if I tried, I'd lose balance, my elbow would wobble, and I'd wind up flat on my back again.

"You're welcome," I said.

"We're going to need to keep moving. The fast ones weren't all that far behind us. Not far behind at all." Josh made sense. Dave, I wasn't a fan.

"Help me up," I said.

Dave and Josh grabbed an arm and hoisted me onto my feet. Allison had an arm around my waist. "I'm good," I said.

They let go. I didn't fall. Wanted to lie down. It would have to wait. That old saying, *there'd be plenty of time to sleep when I'm dead*, came to mind. I didn't speak it out loud. No sense stating the obvious.

"So what's our plan?" Dave said.

"We're going to get my kids."

"We are?"

I shook my head. "No. She and I are. I gave you guys a ride. The truck's totaled. You're on your own."

"On our own to do what? To go where?"

"Chase, we'd like to come with you. There's safety in numbers," Josh said. "Right now, I don't see any benefit to splitting up. I mean, we could, you know. But there's no point."

I took a moment and I closed my eyes again. Just felt better that way. Eyes closed. World lost on the opposite side of the eyelids. I saw nothing but darkness, but that darkness was more than comforting. It felt tranquil.

"He sleeping?" Dave said.

And the tranquility shattered. If Dave was going to journey with them, he needed to learn to keep his mouth shut. I couldn't handle someone without a filter for their words.

"There something seriously wrong with you?" I said.

Dave came at me. Fist raised. Josh stepped between us. I wanted to *deck* the guy. The way my head spun, and his size--at least a hundred pounds more than I was--part of me was silently thankful for the interjection.

Josh pushed Dave back. He turned and looked at me.

"This isn't going to work," I said and waved my hands flaunting discouragement. I was not interested in them tagging along. This was about my kids. And, the more I thought about it, Allison. These guys would slow me down. I didn't need to explain my every move to them. I wasn't going to be looking for permission or a general consensus on what to do next. The shots were mine. I was calling them.

Josh put an arm around my shoulder. He whispered, "Can I talk to you for a second?"

"Are you kidding me?" I shrugged his arm off my body and took a step back. "We're being chased, hunted, by . . . by fucking zombies, dude. Zombies. I don't have the time, the patience or even the fucking desire to give you a second. My kids are home with their zombie-fuck of a mother and her husband. They are in danger. They are holed up somewhere inside that house waiting for me to come and rescue them. Me. Their daddy. A second? Give you a second? Buddy, you and your friend there--"

"He's my brother."

I rolled my eyes. "Go fuck yourselves."

I walked away. Away from Josh. Away from Dave. Away from Allison. I started in the direction I needed to be headed. Talking time was over.

I thought.

Josh fell in step beside me. "My brother, Dave. He is special. Fell when he was young. Our father dropped him in the driveway when he was a baby. His brain swelled. Had part of his skull cut away. It all healed, but he's never been the same. He's not like retarded, but he is special. His mind works a little different. He has trouble figuring out things, or behaving properly. It isn't his fault. So I just wanted to apologize for the things he's said so far. He was out of line, but he doesn't know it. And I don't hold it against you for not wanting us to join the two of you. I respect that. But before we parted, go our separate ways, I just wanted to apologize."

I stood there. Chewed on my lips. Contemplated everything this stranger just said to me. Maybe because I didn't move, Josh felt encouraged to continue. I let him, half listening while I let stuff just sink in. Not just what was being said, but everything. Was like when I closed my eyes and Dave insulted me, only my eyes were open, and I couldn't hear Dave talking.

"Anyway, thanks for picking us up back there. Good luck finding your kids." Josh held his hand out.

"I know where they are."

"Okay." Josh pulled his hand away. "Take care."

Josh walked toward his brother. "We ready?"

Dave showed his palms, raised his shoulders. "What? We ain't going with them?"

"Not this time, Dave."

"So where we going? I mean, what are we supposed to do now? I dropped my bat somewhere. I think when we crashed. I don't even have my bat." Dave walked around in circles, head down, perhaps searching for his lost baseball bat.

I pressed my thumbs against my temples.

"You're sending them away?" Allison stood beside me.

"Sending them away? They're free to do whatever they want. This is ridiculous." I huffed, actually huffed, and through my hands up in surrender. "Alley."

"Chase."

My shoulders deflated. "Josh, wait. Wait up."

The brothers stopped walking. They didn't turn. They didn't start back.

I looked at Allison. "I'm not begging them."

Allison crossed her arms over her chest.

"Really? This falls on me?"

She arched an eyebrow.

"Josh," I said, wasn't yelling. If he didn't hear me, then at least I tried. Alley couldn't be upset with me for trying. "Why don't you guys hang out with us for a while?"

CHAPTER NINETEEN

Didn't take long for the four of us to become thieves.

Traveling close to houses, we kept to the shadows, and at one point, stumbled upon an armory of yard tools. I gave up the hockey stick for a wood handled shovel. Allison stuck the flashlight through a belt loop and retrieved hedge clippers. Josh tucked a hand shovel into each pocket, and carried a hoe like he was an Amazon native armed with a spear. Thing resembled a fireman's *halligan* bar. Dave went all old school with a four-tined pitchfork.

There was no denying it, try as I might. It did feel safer with the four of us. Perhaps it was the additional weapons. More than likely, it was the two extra men, and Dave being a brick wall at that. It wasn't that Allison couldn't handle herself. She was still alive and had proven to me that she could. She'd destroyed the fat zombie that had attacked her from out of the bathroom. No, this was something different. Maybe it was because these two guys didn't mean as much to me. Didn't mean I didn't care, or wouldn't have their back. Just meant, with Alley, it was different. I was too close.

We didn't move house to house, hiding behind bushes. Could have. Instead, we stayed close to houses, and walked across yards. Four wide, instead of one behind the other. We started that way. Taking cover behind anything and everything we could find to take cover behind. When we went ten minutes without seeing a single zombie, we got lax. I knew we'd be using our new garden tools soon. Just wasn't sure when. And relaxed or not, the knot in the pit of my stomach was tied, tight.

My cell phone rang.

We all stopped. I dug it out of my pocket. Hands fumbling. It wasn't just that I was anxious to answer, the ringing sounded like the Liberty Bell tolling in the silence that enveloped the area.

"Chase, the fuck, man?"

I shot Dave a look that should have said, *shut your fucking mouth or I'll use the blade on this shovel to slice your head off your body and bury it deep up your ass.* Must have worked, because he broke eye contact and settled for looking down at the pavement.

It was my daughter. "Char? Charlene?"

"We left the house, Daddy. We had to. Mom, and Donald-- they're sick. They tried to attack us."

"Where is Cash?"

"Here. He's with me." She was sobbing. Her words difficult to understand. The next few words though, I didn't catch them.

"Honey, what? What was that? Where are you?"

"We hid in the garage. Don came out there," she said. "He looked crazy. I told him to stay away. I put Cash behind me. I was protecting him."

"You're an awesome sister, Char."

"But he wouldn't stop. He kept coming at us. I hurt him," she said.

Can't deny it. A bit of pride swelled inside me. Think my chest protruded some to show it, too. "It's okay, honey. These things -- they aren't human. Not anymore. Where are you guys now?"

"I chopped off his hand, Daddy. I used an ax. It was his. It was leaning against the wall. I used it to chop off his hand."

I couldn't imagine. It had to have been a nightmare. She was a kid. Fourteen. Chopping off a hand would disturb me, and I'm as fucked up as they come. "You had to, Charlene. To protect yourself. It's okay. Are you okay?"

A few seconds of sniffling. "I'm--"

The line went dead. "Charlene? Charlene?"

I looked at the phone. Call was dropped. Towers are either working quadruple time or sporadically. And the green bar at the top of the display let me know the phone was not going to last much longer. I should have stopped home; at least I could have thrown some things, including my charger into a backpack.

I redialed her number. Fast busy signal. I disconnected the call. Tried again. Fast busy. I almost threw my phone. Took tons of strength not to. It was the only means of contact with my kids at this point. That single thought kept me from smashing the palm-sized piece of plastic onto the pavement.

Allison had a hand on my shoulder. Might have been there the whole time. "They're not there?"

"They ran. Char and Cash took off. My fucking ex and her husband attacked them." I shook my head. I thought it would be easy to say, that the pride I'd felt would make me want to tell everyone, but the words were trapped in my throat, and sobs of my own sat on top of them. "She used an ax on the guy. Cut off his hand."

"Where did they go?"

"She didn't get to tell me," I said. I swallowed *it*. All of *it*. There'd be a time for *it*, later. Now was not that time. "We're still going to the house. I need to see what's happened."

"You think that's best? We know they are not there." Allison's eyes stared into mine, like she was trying to figure out my motivation for still going to my ex's if the kids were no longer there.

"We're not going anywhere right now, guys." Josh stared straight ahead. A motley crue looking group, a gang of people, filled the streets down near Maiden Lane. It intersected Mt. Read. A gas station, a vacant gas station, a Rite Aid and a small Greek restaurant occupied the four corners. "They're coming this way."

"Slow, jagged movement," Allison said. "Zombies."

"We've got to get off the road. Completely." Josh ran toward the closest house. He tried the knob. "Locked."

He was right. We needed to get into a house. Ride this wave out and hope the monsters just passed by. Best I could tell, there were forty, maybe fifty of them. They seemed different from the other zombies encountered. These appeared organized. Just the way they walked the street together gave off a sense of order, order I didn't like seeing.

"Should we back track?" Dave was looking the way we'd come.

"Try those houses," I said. "Be quiet about it."

Dave took off, running up the porch steps of the house we'd just passed.

"That's the retirement home across the street," Allison said. I looked. "We don't want to be anywhere near there. You know they all got the shot."

I tried a smile. It felt awkward. It wasn't for my benefit. "We're going to find a house. We'll get in--"

"Chase!"

I closed my eyes. Not sure what part of quiet confused Dave. Was it the whole word? The double syllables? I took Allison by the hand. "See, we'll hole up in the house until they pass. Then we'll be on the move again. Won't be in there long at all."

Josh was already running toward the house his brother had found. Allison and I fell in behind him. We stayed in the shadows as best as possible. The zombies coming our way were in the street, under the lights. Hopefully they didn't have vision like cats.

Dave stood on the white porch. He held open the screen door to the house. He waved us in. It was the shit-ass stupid grin he wore that made me want to pop him in the mouth. Tried to remember the fact that he wasn't right in the head. "Good job," I said, instead of a knuckle sandwich. The guy beamed.

Once inside, we shut the door, engaged the locks.

"We need to clear the place," Josh said.

"What?" Allison looked from Josh to me.

"He's right. Before we go boarding up windows and locking doors. We have no idea who might be in here."

With the little moonlight available or it was a street light, I don't know--don't care, I saw Dave's fingers on the wall.

"Don't touch the lights," I said.

"But we can't see anything," he said.

"David, leave the lights off."

I looked outside. The zombies were not walking as slow as I'd thought. They weren't directly outside the house we'd hidden in, but they were close.

"I have this." Allison pulled the flashlight out of her belt loop. "The batteries died, but if we can find some?"

And then the living room we were all in, went bright. Lit up.

Allison cursed, and fumbled with the flashlight. "They were dead," she said, switching the light off. "They didn't work before."

"Shit," I said. I had been looking out the window, fingers slightly parting thin drapes. "One of those things is . . . ah shit. They're coming this way."

"The zombies?"

"No, Dave. The pizza guy. I placed an order when I knew we were going to be here for a while," I said. No idea if Dave grasped sarcasm. Didn't seem to. Part of me thought he was dying to ask what toppings I got on the pie.

"He's right," Josh said. "We don't have time to clear the place. We have to lock it down. Good."

"This picture window is huge."

"Everyone just be quiet. Shhh." I said. "Josh, you and Dave go look for a back door. Stay there. If things go bad out here, and as long as it stays clear back there, we're going to need a way out. Fast. And Josh?"

He stopped. "Yeah?"

"Stay low, away from windows. We can't be making a lot of noise. Right now, I think the only thing we got on our side is the flimsy locks on the doors. They start breaking windows, we're running for it. And Josh?"

"Huh?"

"Allison, give him your radio," I said. "They make a lot of static, Josh. Only use it if you have to. And Josh?"

He cocked a hip and sighed at me. "Yeah?"

"Take Dave," I said.

"I don't like this," Allison said when we were alone. "This seems worse than when we were in the security office."

I didn't have time to compare dire situations. The stairs that led upstairs were directly behind the front door. "Stand behind me. Watch the stairs."

"Watch them for what?"

I put my shoulder against the door. "Don't be stupid."

I pressed my eye to the peephole. At least one of those things most definitely saw Allison turn on the flashlight. But not all of them. They were all off the street now. Forty, fifty of them. And they were on the lawn. They were walking right toward the front window.

"Don't make a sound."

CHAPTER TWENTY

We were locked inside a house. We might not be alone. The zombies outside saw us in here. It was accidental, I know. Alley should have known better than to switch on the flashlight, even if she thought the batteries were dead. Now we were split up. Josh and Dave were somewhere in the back of this place, hopefully by an exit, keeping an eye out for creatures back there, while Allison and I had the front door blocked and were silently hopeful the things would lose interest and continue their trek south down Mt. Read. Too bad there wasn't any traffic. Would love seeing the lot of them struck by vehicles.

This was not the time for day dreaming, or wishful thinking.

"Chase," Allison whispered.

"Shhh."

"Chase," she said, again.

I turned away from the peephole. Turned away from scouting the area on the opposite side of the door. Turned away from watching most of the zombies move on, finding nothing but what must have appeared to them like a vacant house. "What?"

Allison had her arms held out in front of her. Holding the Y handle of her hedge clippers in a white-knuckle grip. "We're not alone."

It was a whisper. I heard her as if she'd yelled. I looked up the stairs. Hairs on my arm stood. A cold sweat broke out on my skin. A shudder passed down my spine. "Ah, shit," I said.

It was like something out of a horror film. The old woman at the top of staircase stood still in a white nightie that reached to just above her ankles. Ruffles around the cuffs and neckline. Pale, decayed skin was the flesh that covered her skull and was her face. Her arms were at her side. She didn't appear to have any fingers on one hand. Made me think if she was the only one in the house, she might have eaten the digits herself.

"We need to stay quiet," I said. "Watch the door. Don't make a sound."

Allison and I swapped spots. I wanted her to keep an eye at the peephole. I had my back to her. I knew she was watching me and the woman at the top of the stairs, regardless. Suppose I would be too.

I held my shovel; the rounded end aimed at the woman, as if it were a spear, and walked up the first stair.

"What are you doing?" Allison had her hand on my shoulder.

"She has to go."

"It's her house."

I ignored that stupid comment and took another step closer. The woman just stood there. She wasn't swaying. She wasn't moaning. Had she been glowing, I'd of sworn she was a ghost and not a zombie. And on a night like tonight, I'd have easily accepted a haunting. Easily.

"Watch the peep hole," I said. My eyes never left the woman. There was no way to gauge her age. The peeling flesh on her cheeks and milky white eyeballs made it impossible. Only thing I had was the tuft of thin white hair rolled in curlers and held in place with a yellow and blue bandanna. No one did that anymore, just old people did.

Seven steps separated us. The blade of the shovel would reach her in two. I held the wood handle with both hands. Sweat coated my palms. I gripped and re-gripped as I took another step. With a jab, I think I could reach her from here, without having to get any closer. I needed the striking blow to deliver death. Not just knock her back, or cut into her. Like it or not, I' have to shave more off the distance between us.

It was the way she just stood there, though. Staring. Vacant. She didn't seem anxious, or hungry to eat me. Drool, or puss, or nothing fell from her lips. If she wasn't a ghost, I'd put money on poorly crafted mannequin, way before I guessed flesh eating zombie.

I pulled the shovel back, so I could strike fast and hard with some momentum as I climbed the next step. Sweat was behind my knees. I felt more apprehensive about this one. I'd killed a few along the way. Maybe because the few I'd killed put my life in immediate danger. Or Allison's. And at this point, Mannequin has not made as much as an aggressive flinch.

She freaked me the fuck out, but I didn't feel threatened. Yet.

Would her freaking me out be reason enough to destroy her skull? She was not human. That was clear. Evident in the black goo that dripped from stumps that used to contain at least eight fingers and a few thumbs. You sever parts of the body, you bleed. Blood. Red blood. Not goo. Black goo.

We were in danger. We were. A flock of zombies were on the lawn. Enveloping the house--Mannequin's house. They did not seem to be interested enough to force entry. Had a feeling if they suspected four . . . humans were inside, they might. The way they'd appeared all gang-like and organized, I couldn't put past them that it wouldn't take much to realize breaking glass would be as good as opening a door. Mannequin had to go. Just like I'd said when I'd climbed up the first step. Whether that had been for Allison's sake or mine, did not matter.

Feeling like a coiled rattler, and just as I was ready to lunge springing forward to chop Mannequin to death, the radio on my hip squawked and hissed. I stared down at it.

"Chase? What's it like out front. Clear back here."

My jaw dropped open. Fucking Dave. Josh gave Dave the fucking radio.

"Chase!" Allison said.

I looked up the stairs. Mannequin was gone. Just, gone.

Shit. Now what. "I have to find her. Please, Alley, keep a lookout." I took the radio off my hip, handed it down to her. "Turn down the volume, and answer that fuck."

"You're going up there?"

"Unless you saw her pass me on the stairs and she's hiding down here somewhere? Did you see her do that? Did you see her pass me? Is she down here?"

"You don't have to be a dick," she said.

I gave her my back, re-gripped my hold on the shovel and climbed the stairs into a windowless and completely pitch black hallway. "Ah, shit."

I could barely see a thing in front of me. I strained to listen. Thought I might hear Mannequin breathing, or groaning, or something. But nothing. Not a sound. About the only thing I heard was my own heartbeat. It filled my ears with a muffled *tha-thump, tha-thump*, and my own heavy breathing. I might not hear Mannequin, but if she wasn't deaf with old age, she'd hear me.

Don't know if it was strength or courage I conjured, but taking that first step was not easy. Still, I took it. Each step after -- no easier.

I had to take one hand off the shovel to feel along the wall. I was looking for a door, or doorway. Last thing I wanted to feel, but the one thing that kept coming to mind, was the touch of a cotton nightie. I shivered.

My fingers grazed over fuzzy wallpaper. Reminded me of mold. I almost pulled my hand away. Instead, I pushed forward. Seemed like I'd covered more than a hundred yards. A chanced look back told me maybe I'd crossed a foot or two. The baby steps weren't getting the job done.

Molding. A doorway. I felt around. The door was open. I reached across to the opposite wall, the wall on the east and touched fuzziness. So no one was behind me. I took a deep breath. Held it, and sent the end of my shovel into the room ahead of me. I poked and jabbed at air. Followed in close behind. I swung it back and forth, just to make sure Mannequin wasn't standing right there, waiting for me.

She wasn't. The window across the room let in some outside light. I could turn on the light. Josh and Dave had indicated the back yard was clear. This room faced that direction. I didn't want to risk it. Didn't seem worth it. Instead, I stood at the threshold a moment, hoping my eyes would adjust. I didn't have all night. A few extra seconds wasn't going to hurt, especially if it helped my sight.

Or so I thought.

CHAPTER TWENTY-ONE

There should have been a warning. Some kind of sound. I should have smelled the decaying flesh. Instead, I tried to jump back as stumps where fingers should have been slammed into my back, sending me forward, reeling. My eyes adjusted to the darkness as I lost balance and stumbled toward the bed.

Under the covers lie a man. What was once a man. Best I could tell, it had been a man. If his face had been green, he'd of resembled a watermelon sliced in half and eaten by a dog. Nose, mouth and upper jaw . . . gone. So was most of the brain. His face looked more like a bowl. A deep, hollowed out hole. Only thing that told me it was a male, was the pajama top. Mannequin was in an old-fashioned nightgown, and this old guy wore pajamas. Didn't think people wore that kind of stuff anymore.

And then I was on him. Chests criss-crossing. I smelled him. Insides reeked, emptied bowels mashed by the extra weight of me *on* the deceased.

Before I could push off, or roll off of the dead guy, Mannequin was on me, fell or dropped onto my back. Envisioning those gooey stumps slapping at me, as if trying to get a finger grasp on my shirt, or to dig fingernails into my skin for a hold, had me bucking like a bull that did not want to be ridden.

I felt trapped, pinned between two bodies. The shovel useless, sandwiched like this. I'd seen enough horror movies to know I was in some shit. Had no idea if getting bit infected me with whatever *they* had. Would I become one of them? That thought alone had my own bowels ready to release.

Unlike when I first entered the room, I heard her. Mannequin. She breathed hard and heavy. Like an excited woman. She seemed to be scaling my back. Perhaps getting her head in position to chomp down on my exposed and highly vulnerable neck.

This kicked my adrenaline into hyper-drive. I thrashed. Twisted. I was not going to be bitten, but neither was I able to throw her off my back.

Her hot breath was on my skin. Near my neck.

The inevitable happened. I felt a prick on my shoulders. Sharp teeth sinking into my flesh. I screamed. Couldn't help it.

"I got her," I heard.

Dave.

All at once, the weight was lifted off me. The sound of a body hitting the floor followed. I rolled over, and off of the dead man. In the dimly lit room, I saw Dave. He stood with a two-handed grip on his pitchfork.

I sat up, looked down. The tines of his weapon had pierced Mannequin's head. He stepped on her back and pulled free the pitchfork. My hand went to my neck. There was some bleeding. Warm, and sticky. "I think she bit me," I said. I felt sick. Thought I might throw up. I had no clue what was in store.

"Let me see," Dave said. He slapped a hand on my shoulder and spun me around. "My bad."

"What's your bad?"

"She didn't bite you. The pitchfork went too far. I think those marks are from this," he said, and held up his weapon.

"Not a bite?"

"Doesn't look like it."

I wanted to cry. Relief washed through me. My shoulders deflated. I sighed. And sighed again. "Oh my, God. Thank you. Thank you."

"For stabbing you?"

New respect for the slow man filled me. I stood up. Put out my hand. "For saving my life."

He shook it. "It was nothing. You saved ours earlier. It's what friends do."

I'd not had many opportunities to save lives. Of friends, or otherwise. There was the one time a guy was choking on a mouth full of french fries at Schaller's. I performed the Heimlich. He spat a wad of chewed potato across the room, but he was breathing, and alive. "I suppose in days like this, it is. I appreciate it."

I wanted to apologize for being a dick, but figured I'd wait it out. See what type of friendship actually blossomed.

"Josh is watching the back. Allison's at the front door still. She was worried. I came to apologize about the radio. She told me you were up here. That there was one of those things up here. I didn't want you to go at it alone. Thought I might be able to help. Have your back, you know?"

"I'm glad you did. Again, thank you." I looked around the room. My shovel was on the opposite side of the bed. I walked around to retrieve it.

"She musta ate her husband?"

"Looks that way."

"This is fucked up, you know? I mean, seriously fucked up shit."

"Tell me about it." I clapped him on the back. "Let's check the rest of the rooms up here. Just make sure there aren't any more surprises."

"Good call."

We cleared a second bedroom and bathroom at the end of the hallway. There was a door that led to an attic. We looked at each other. Chance of this old couple having more people in the attic did not seem plausible. Dave volunteered to give it a once-over. I stopped him. "Let me," I said.

A thin cord dangled just over the third step. Didn't suspect the attic had windows. I chanced the light and pulled the cord. A naked bulb bounced and swung back and forth from the tug. It cast moving shadows in every corner of the attic. With just my head at floor level, I prairie-dogged it. Gave the room a full 360. Aside from neatly stacked and black marker-labeled boxes, no one was hiding in the attic. Relieved, I turned off the light and went back down the stairs.

"Anything?"

"Nothing. Clear."

CHAPTER TWENTY-TWO

Josh and I sat at the kitchen table. Dave had raided the fridge, found left over deep fried chicken and a saran wrapped bowl of mashed potatoes. He pulled a few cans of French cut green beans from the cabinet, added some Italian salad dressing to it, and together, and in silence, we ate a meal.

The front lawn was loaded with what seemed like camped-out zombies. They didn't seem to be going anywhere. They wondered up and down the driveway, went around the side of the house and explored the backyard, came back and walked up and down the driveway.

It was 4 a.m. We'd sent Dave and Allison to sleep on sofas in the family room about an hour a half ago. No sense all of us staying up. Josh told me to get some sleep too, but I wasn't interested. When there was a break in zombies, I wanted to be ready to run. Thought it might have lasted a half hour or so. Never expected them to remain.

My gut was in knots. I'd eaten, but feared I'd not be able to keep the food down. It went down easy. Stayed down, too. Mannequin had been an amazing cook.

I held a portrait of Mannequin and her husband. They were a cute old couple. I'd put them in their late 70's. The way they sat close posing, and the natural smiles they wore, spoke volumes. They were side-by-side on a wood swing bench with an umbrella awning. Behind them was a body of water. Could be Lake Ontario. Didn't have to be. The sun set on the horizon. The colors were spectacular. The entire photograph made the viewer feel warm and serene. I was half-tempted to go through their things, not just pull the framed photo off the mantel. I wanted to know who they were. Their names, at the very least.

But I also didn't want to know shit about them.

I set the frame down, the photo facing the table.

I'd seen and learned enough. They were gone. Dead. Together.

"So," I said, if only to break the silence between us. "You and Dave, you guys from Rochester?"

"Yeah, actually."

"Family?"

"No. Parents died. Our mother battled cancer most of her life. Lost to it when Dave was around thirteen. Hit our father pretty hard. He sank into a depression. Five years later, to the day--a massive heart attack took him. It's been Dave and me since then."

"No aunts, uncles."

"Couple of each. They were cool to us. Wanted us to visit, and stuff. No one offered to take us in. We were old enough to be on our own and everything. But, with Dave--it hasn't been easy. He struggles keeping a job. You might not have noticed, but he's an adult, and he's a handful." Josh snickered. I did too.

"Tell me more about Mexico," Josh said.

We sat in darkness, across from each other. My eyes were so adjusted to the darkness I felt like a cat.

"The government put up that huge wall to keep aliens out of our country," I said.

"Right, sure."

"Now the Mexican government is using it to keep us out of their country. The infected anyway. I'm guessing they got guards watching it. Making sure none of us sneak in."

"You know all of this how?"

"There was something on the radio. Late yesterday. Said something like, the Mexicans couldn't afford to vaccinate their residents. Or there wasn't enough vaccination to go around. Something like that. So it's an uninfected country with an amazing border wall that we installed. Like a fucking fortress, their country," I said.

Even in darkness, I saw it. His head nodded. But he was looking down at his folded hands on the table.

"What?"

"I mean, theoretically it sounds good."

"What does that mean? I heard it. It's what they said."

"What channel? Who said it?"

"Why is it so hard to believe, Josh?" I said.

"Why is it so easy to believe?"

"I don't know what your issue is. Yeah, okay. Mexico is a few thousand miles away. Roads are shit. But we're going there. We're not infected. We're going to cross the border, and start a new life."

"We are?"

This time I shook my head. "My kids and I. You guys can come."

"The bulk of the outbreak seems to have occurred today, well, yesterday now -- since the sun's about to rise."

"Seems that way. Yeah."

"But I don't think yesterday was the very first day. I've watched the news. All kinds of weird shit was happening across the country the day before. Remember there was that guy on the expressway, was naked, eating some cab drivers face ... right out on the road, stopped traffic up for hours."

"So?"

"That happened in Dallas."

"Okay, Dallas. Josh, either you have a fucking point, or you don't."

"No point." He stood up.

I slammed my fists on the table. "What was the point, Josh?"

"We're starting a third day here," he pointed toward the front of the house. As if he could see a rising sun, or something. I knew what he meant. He was indicating a new day was dawning.

"Yeah, and?"

"And, just think about it. Planes. Cars passing through the border. Thousands of cars pass through that border every day. There's no way the country doesn't have infected people in it. Just, there isn't. This is clearly an epidemic. I'd say turn the TV on, let's hear what they're saying, but right now might not be the best time." Josh walked out of the kitchen. End of conversation.

I sat there. Thinking.

Shit if he didn't actually have a point.

# # #

Hands on my shoulders woke me. I jumped up. I'd fallen asleep at the table.

"We're going to move." Allison knelt beside me.

"They're gone?" I said.

"All of them. Not sure when, or how long, but they've moved on."

"What time is it?"

"Noon." I looked around the kitchen. Sunlight filled the house, even with curtains pulled closed. "Why'd you let me sleep so long?"

"You needed it," Josh said.

"We all did." Allison stood. "There's coffee."

A cup of coffee and a cigarette sounded amazing. Sounded normal. I pulled my cell phone out of my pocket. No *missed* anything. I dialed my daughter's number. Fast busy signal. "Everyone's ready?"

"We are," Josh said. "Want to take a fast shower?"

I looked up at the kitchen ceiling. Remembered what was upstairs. A shower sounded better than coffee and a cigarette. "I'm going to pass," I said.

Josh said, "How far, exactly, to your kids?"

I looked at Allison. Knew what she was thinking. They weren't there last time I talked to Charlene. They'd had to flee. My daughter was using an ax. "Near the lake. Big house, at the end of Dewey."

Josh looked like he'd swallowed his tongue. "That's still a few miles."

"We should try and get another car."

"Bet the people that lived here have one." Dave started opening drawers.

"What are you doing?" I asked.

"Car keys. They must be around here."

By the phone on the wall near the back door was a key chain rack. I walked over, lifted a set off the hook. "Like here?"

Dave beamed. "Exactly."

I shook my head. Was going to be a long day.

We stopped at the garage door. I pressed an ear to the wood. Behind me, they were all ready with their garden tool weapons. "On three," I said.

As slowly as possible, I disengaged the deadbolt. I turned the lock on the knob, and then pulled open the door.

Dark, but clearly empty. Where was the car?

"The driveway?" Allison said.

Made sense. They had car keys. There must be a car. If not in the garage, then in the driveway. We left the kitchen. Walked in a line.

Allison smelled like Pert Shampoo. She'd showered. I must smell like shit.

Three of us huddled between the front door and staircase. Josh stood by the picture window. With the back of one hand, he parted the curtain and chanced a look outside.

"Well?" I said.

"Still looks clear."

"We should go, then. While we have the chance," Dave said. He looked at me and nodded. His tongue might as well be dangling out of the corner of his mouth, and his nose wet. That's how much he reminded me of a giant sheep dog.

"I agree, but maybe now is the best time to try the television. See what the news is saying." Josh let the curtain fall closed.

He also stared at me. Got the feeling if I said, No, that would be the end of it. And we'd venture outdoors, blind.

"Good idea. Keep it low. Very, very low," I said.

Dave walked toward the couch.

"Uh-huh, Dave. We're staying right here. By the door. Away from the windows," I said. "We can see the set fine from here."

Josh stayed low. He squatted in front of the television and turned it on.

We all stared as he flipped through channels of nothing but white-snow-static.

Until he stopped on what seemed to be the only channel still . . . alive and working.

CHAPTER TWENTY-THREE

Fox News Reporter, Jeremy Thomas sat in front of a green screen. A helicopter's view of Washington was displayed behind him. Chaos ensued on the White House grounds. Secret Service used automatic rifles to fire strings of shots at zombies.

"Recent reports indicate that the President is safe. While the nation's capital is under attack, both the president and vice president have been taken to separate secure undisclosed locations. All branches of the military are working together to combat the common enemy. It is advised that everyone remain indoors until the situation is controlled. Phone lines are down. Cellular towers are working, but sporadically. The National Guard and all branches of the military have been deployed on US soil. Safe-compounds are being set up in the following states and cities. . ."

Static - white snow. The signal lost.

Josh banged the TV.

It was a flat screen. It did nothing to fix the picture. Instead, it wobbled on its base and fell forward.

"What the fuck, Josh," Dave said. I couldn't have said it any better.

Josh picked the set up. Set it back on the stand. The screen was not broken. White snow filled every bit of the 52 inches.

"Check through the channels again," Allison said.

Josh had the remote pointed at the cable box, and was scrolling. "Nothing. We got nothing."

At first, I thought it looked and sounded hopeless. I'll admit the US military never entered my mind. They were a positive ray. If anyone could thin out the heard of zombies, those boys could. Would. It wouldn't be easy, but they had the training and weapons.

"Where do you think these camps are?" Allison said.

"I'll bet one is in D.C.," Josh said. "Probably one somewhere in New York, too."

"But we don't know where," I said. "Let's look around. See if this couple had a transistor radio. My guess is they will. And batteries. That will at least give us some way of keeping a pulse on what's happening."

"It's a good idea," Josh said.

We scattered. The scavenger hunt had begun.

Then something exploded.

The house shook.

Allison screamed.

We all ran back into the living room.

"You okay?" I asked, looking at everyone.

"It came from outside," Dave said, pointing at the picture window.

I peeked out. I couldn't see anything. "I'm going out," I said.

"We don't know what that was," Allison said.

"It's why I have to check," I said.

I had my shovel. "Lock this door as soon as you shut it, got it?"

She nodded. I didn't believe her. "Dave, you make sure this door is locked once I'm outside."

"You got it," he said.

I stepped out onto the front step. Didn't need to go much further to notice three things. There was no car in the driveway, and the house next door was on fire. Colorful flames licked at the afternoon sky. Heat rolled off the burning clapboard and hit me like a wave in the face and chest. Third, the loud boom from the explosion was bringing curious zombies out of the woodwork. They were still a ways off, but they were coming.

I turned, knocked on the door.

"Who is it?"

"Fuckin', Dave, let me in!"

The door opened. I'd only just stepped outside. Josh said his brother was a bit slow, but this was a bit ridiculous. He might have saved my life last night, but I'd bet money he'd also be the cause of my death. "We have to get out of here."

"What was it?" Josh held a plastic bag in his hands.

"House next door. Gone. Coulda been a natural gas leak. Which means, we're not safe in here. Not anymore," I said. "The gas lines run from house to house. No fire department is coming and RG&E isn't going to shut the gas off, if you know what I mean." I started toward the kitchen, and back door. They followed.

"What about the car?" Josh said.

"Isn't one."

"Where is it?" Dave asked.

I ignored him. "Zombies are coming back. The sound. It calls them. Noise does. So we have to be fast, and we have to be quiet. Shut the two-ways off."

Josh and Allison switched off the radios.

"I don't think staying close to the houses is going to be smart. Not right now. We need to put some distance between us."

Another explosion, then two smaller ones rattled the walls of the house we were in.

"What was that?" Allison said.

"We have to move, now."

In a line, me at the front, Allison behind me, followed by Dave and Josh, we moved like a snake towards the back of the yard. Going around front didn't make sense, it was where I had seen the gathering of walking dead. Running through yards and jumping fences didn't seem easy either, but right now, it was the only option I could think of.

The other explosion was another house. The two, side by side, were now fully engulfed. Black smoke rolled into the air. Inside the houses, white sparks and pops sounded. It was loud. The roar of the fire was deafening. Glass broke inside. Shattered. Sounded like ceilings caving, or staircases crumbling. Even at the edge of the yard, we could feel the heat. I don't know how firemen run inside those things, wearing all that gear, and breathing into a tiny face mask.

"Over the fence?" Allison said.

"Yep. Over," I said.

Dave went first. We handed him our garden tools. I hoisted Allison up and over next. Josh and I climbed at the same time.

We landed in the next yard. The in-ground pool was covered. Cinder blocks held the cover in place. A tiny two-person gazebo sat alone between the pool and the back patio. Nice place. Probably had a house full of zombies inside trying to figure out how to open a door.

"Keep moving," I said. "This house could blow at any time."

"Should we keep following the gas line? I mean, stay on Mt. Read, or should we cut back? Go toward the street behind this one. What is it?"

"True Hickory," Allison said.

"We could. We just follow it, and cut through the bit of woods at the end. Wind up in the Tops Friendly Market parking lot," I said. "Okay. Let's do that."

I wasn't looking for a vote. We went kiddie-corner to the back fence, and repeated the jumping over process.

Once on the other side, we knelt in a huddled circle. "With all these trees, we've got some cover. We're not as visible. Let's try staying away from the house, away from noise, and keep back here. Think we'll be able to move faster. Once we get to Tops, I'll figure out what next," I said.

No arguments. All three nodded.

Sneaking through the backyards under the cover of trees was completely different from walking on streets, or sidewalks, or close to houses. This just felt fucking creepy.

Most of the Maples had lost their leaves. Every step sounded like a gunshot when crunching down on dried out foliage, and I cringed. It couldn't be as loud as I thought. But we *were* making noise as we made our way north toward the parking lot. Pines were full, and their branches would soon sport clumps of snow.

Thankfully, it was a chilly November morning -- God, it was now November -- but it was not snowing. The morning air had a bite to it. At this point, it felt invigorating. Got the blood pumping.

I held up a fist. Squatted low.

Allison bumped into me.

I looked at her, at my fist and rolled my eyes.

"Really?" I said.

Josh and Dave had stopped.

"What?" Allison looked at me, head cocked to one side. Her dog-face, I always called it. Confused puppy.

"The fist. See how I have it in the air? How I stopped?"

"I see it."

"It means stop," I said.

"What does?" she said.

"The fist. When I do this. It means stop."

"Says who?" She looked at Josh for support, but Josh nodded in agreement. "You knew this?"

"Even I knew it," Dave said, laughed -- came out more as a chortle, with a pig-like snort at the end.

Josh drove an elbow into his brother's gut. "You want to wake the dead?" He looked at me, half a smile.

Good attempt. Not funny. I ignored him. "You ever see a movie in your life, Alley? I mean, I know, remember we saw that Gulf War movie just like in July, or August? Remember when they were going in to attack the enemy and the squad leader did this, with his fist? And his whole platoon stopped. They just, they stopped?"

"You mean that two and half hour movie, the two seconds of film you're referring to, do I remember it? No, Chase. You wanted to see that movie not me. I think I had my phone under my shirt and was on Twitter through most of it."

Bang, zoom. Was all I could think. "Tell ya what. You see me hold up a fist, if any of us holds up a fist, if you, Alley, if you hold up a fist. We stop. We get low. We be quiet. Deal?"

"If you'd of said that before you became the squadron leader, we wouldn't of had this terrible miscommunication. So why did we stop," Allison said.

I looked forward. Looked around. "Shit."

"Shit, what?" she said.

"I had something important to say."

"But you don't remember now?"

I gritted my teeth. Grounded them. "Let's get to the parking lot."

CHAPTER TWENTY-FOUR

I held up a fist. Everyone stopped, was quiet.

"I remembered," I said. "When we get to the parking lot, we're not just going to cross it. We're going to check it out, find the best way to move back out in the open."

Allison gave me a look. She didn't say it, but her eyes said, *Duh.*

"What's that?" Dave pointed.

I followed that direction. Something was behind one of the pine trees. I clearly saw jeans and boots protruding.

"They could be dead," I said.

The left leg moved.

We all flinched. "Shit. Okay. Dave, Josh, you guys go around to the left. Allison and I will approach straight on. Not a sound."

The . . . forest . . . was thicker the closer we got to Tops. It was harder and harder to see the backs of houses on either our left or right. We were in the middle of the thicket.

Allison and I did the leapfrog thing again. Moving from tree to tree. We were extra careful about where we stepped. A snapped twig, a pile of crunchy leaves, and our stealthy converging would be blown.

Allison moved ahead of me. Stopped by a fat round Maple. She pressed her back to the tree. She held up a fist.

I waited.

She looked at me, brow furrowed. She waved me to her.

I walked as silently as possible.

"I did this," she said, holding up her fist.

"I know. I stopped."

"But I didn't want you to stop back there. I wanted you up here."

I pursed my lips. Hoped they looked like I was smiling and nodded. "What?"

"It's a kid. A teenager. Doesn't look like a zombie."

I peeked around the tree we hid behind. I could see the kid. The teen. He now had his arms wrapped around knees pressed to his chest. He was shivering.

I looked, saw Josh and Dave. Held up a fist.

The fist was getting old.

They stopped though.

"They coming over here?" Allison asked.

"No," I said. "They're not." Her head went to one side.

"What are we going to do?"

"Cover me. Just in case he attacks. Be ready." I stepped away from the tree. I held my arms up, the shovel in one hand, blade down.

I took steps toward the large pine.

"Hey?" I said. "Hey, kid."

He was alert. Might be cold, but he wasn't sleeping. He jumped to his feet.

I hadn't noticed the Glock earlier. He held it in both hands. The barrel aimed at me. From where I stood, about ten yards away, looked like a head shot for sure. I raised my hands higher. "We're not zombies," I said.

"What do you want?"

"We're just passing through."

The kid looked left, right, real fast like. If his peripheral vision focused on anything, I'd of been surprised. He was checking his surroundings, didn't blame him.

Wish he didn't have a gun pointed at me. "We just want to get past you. No trouble."

"We? How many of you are there?"

I didn't want to throw us all under the bus, nor did I want to throw Alley under there either. "Two," I said. "My girlfriend. She's hiding. Doesn't like guns."

"Tell her to come out. I want to see her. How do I know she doesn't have a gun pointed at my head?"

"She doesn't."

"But I don't know that, do I?" He had to be about sixteen. Maybe seventeen. Aside from his jeans and work boots, he had on a grey hoodie over a maroon Greece Cardinals Football shirt and jean jacket. He wore the hood. I couldn't see his eyes. They were overcast in shadows. I couldn't see much else, actually, beyond the front of the handgun pointed at me. "Put the shovel down, and have her come out."

"I am not going to have her come out. She's not a threat."

"Put the shovel down."

"Not going to do that, either kid. And stop yelling. Your voice is going to attract zombies, all right."

"I'll raise me voice and you can't do shit about it."

"I can't," I said. "Not from here. Not with you aiming your gun at me. But he can."

"He can, who?"

"Behind you."

The kid laughed. "I look like a fucking moron?"

"I don't want to see you get hurt. We want nothing from you. We just want to pass by. But if you don't lower the gun, you're going to get hurt."

"I'm not turning around. You'll charge me."

"From here?" I laughed, quietly, shook my head. "I don't think so. But then again, I don't need to charge you."

"Oh, right. Because, 'he' is going to stop me," he said.

"That's right."

"Why don't you go f--"

Dave swung in a swooping arc the handle of the pitchfork. It slammed onto the kid's forearm.

I worried the kid might misfire.

Instead, the Glock fell from his hand.

The kid screamed, cradled the limp wrist close to his body. "The fuck," he said.

Josh tackled him. Threw a hand over the kid's mouth.

Yeah. I'd lied to him about how many we were. But not about just wanting to pass by, not about not wanting anything from him. It didn't have to go down this way. "Get up," I said.

Josh pushed off the kid and stood up.

"You, too," I said. "Up."

He'd stopped yelling, but still clung to his hand. "He broke my wrist."

"I don't think so," Dave said.

I knelt by the kid. "Let me see."

He held out his arm. His hand dangled. His wrist was red, swollen. I felt around the bones. He winced.

"Might have," I said.

"I'm right handed. What the hell am I supposed to do now?" the kid said. I helped him sit up.

"Why did you point a gun at us?" Allison knelt next to me.

"I don't know who you guys are," he said. Nothing tough about his voice. "I lost everyone. Those things, those zombies killed my parents and my little brother. I barely got out of the house. I tried to help them; I grabbed my dad's gun out of the desk in his study. But he never kept it loaded. So I had to find the key to unlock the box in the closet that had the ammo. By then. . ."

The kid cried. Lowered his head to his knees and cried.

Allison touched his shoulder. He shrugged away her hand. She moved closer, sat beside him and wrapped an arm around him. He leaned into her, cried with his head against her chest.

I looked at Josh and Dave, who both stared at Allison and the kid.

I checked the Glock. Had 2 bullets in it. It was one of the newer clips, following the laws that made it illegal to have more than 5 bullets in a handgun. Five bullets would help about as much as the two in this one.

"You can come with us," I said. "We can't leave you alone. Not with a broken wrist. You'll be defenseless. And this," I set the gun down next to the kid. "This will not save you from much. Take down two zombies with head-shots if you've got awesome aim."

The kid sniffled, lifted his head off my girlfriend's breasts and drew the sleeve of his jean jacket under his nose. "Where are you guys going?"

CHAPTER TWENTY-FIVE

The kid decided to join us. We were up to five, with me. I didn't mind, but there were issues with growing. We'd be louder. We were more obvious. There was a chance for more bickering, head-butting, and arguments. It would be easier for one of them to slow us down. The kid was already injured. He had the Glock, with two shots left, but he wasn't going to be able to swing a shovel, or baseball bat, or anything. As it was now, we didn't just have to get past the Tops parking lot, we had to enter the grocery store. Allison wanted to splint the kid's wrist.

I started to argue, but stopped. It was me that asked him to join us. I can't *then* complain that we'll help fix the broken bones we caused. It was his fault; I'm not apologizing for that. He had the gun trained on me. A splint was the least we could do. And the most.

"We're going into the store. Those doors don't lock. It's open twenty-four hours. So there's bound to be zombies inside," I said, thinking of the mall.

"Parking lot looks clear," Allison said.

We were huddled close together at the edge of the shallow woods. Thick brush kept us hidden. We had a clear view of the parking lot. A few cars were in an array of spaces. Allison was right, though. No sign of zombies. Didn't mean they weren't close. Best I could tell though, we had a straight shot for the entrance without hurdles.

Thing that came to mind was whether we should all go, or just two of us. Once inside, we could easily be challenged, and wind up trapped. Needless to get everyone killed. At the same time, I did not want to be killed. Seemed I was the only one with somewhere to be, somewhere to go. It was my idea to get a splint and gauze. I had to be one of those entering the store.

"I'm going to go," I said. "I want you guys to wait here."

"I'm going with you," Allison said.

"Us, too," Josh volunteered.

"I'm not staying out here alone," the kid said.

"What's your name," I said.

"Me?" the kid pointed at himself. "Jay. Jason."

"All right, Jay. We're all going to stay close. Josh, I'll take point. I want you to follow us, but stay outside the store. Looks clear enough. But if a big group of zombies comes this way, I want you to be able to warn us with enough time to get out of the store. Know what I mean? Watch out backs."

Josh nodded.

"Allison, I want Jay behind me. You behind him. Dave, you follow Allison." I scanned the parking lot again. Still looked good. "We are going to run close to the building, right through the automated doors. Good?"

We left cover and crossed the delivery road that led to the back of the grocery store. My eyes felt like they were seizing, looking everywhere all at once. Surprised I didn't get dizzy.

I'd seen *Zombieland*. And while it was funny seeing the two main guys banjo-playing while checking a grocery store for Zingers, I was not enjoying myself. I knew the Tops layout. Knew the First Aid supplies would be near the M&T Bank, all the way to the left. Past the checkout stations, by the beer.

We reached the entrance. "You got us?"

Josh nodded. "Go, go."

We went through the automated doors, into the foyer with the rows of metal shopping carts, and newspaper racks, we stopped. Quick pow-wow.

"If it looks safe, Alley, I want you to hit the school supply aisle. See if you can't grab a couple of back backs. If we can load up on some essentials while we're here, then we should." I was staring into her eyes. They weren't the same as before. I wouldn't believe it, if I wasn't seeing it. They'd hardened. Looked cold. She was a different, stronger person. I trusted her. She'd proven herself time and again.

"I'll take Dave," she said.

Was a good call.

"Kid, you come with me."

"Jay," he said.

"Whatever. Just stay close. Right behind me, and not a sound. Alley, you make as much noise as you have to if something goes wrong," I said.

"Got it."

"We'll meet back at the first check out. The one closest to the exit. Okay? Turn your radio on, Alley. Just keep the volume low." I switched mine on, as well.

"It's for emergencies only," Dave said.

"Right," I said, "let's be quick about this."

Around the corner was the huge shopping center. Produce and meats to the right. General groceries and seasonal items straight ahead. Frozen foods, refrigerated items and beverages, pet supplies, snacks, paper goods, health and beauty, and First Aid stuff to the left.

It was hard not to imagine shopping as a family. When the kids were little, my ex and I shopped together. Actually looked forward to it. The kids acted like they were at Disney World. We'd stop at the bakery first. Pass up food we planned to buy, in order to get to the bakery. Charlene and Cash wanted their free cookie. There was a Tupperware container by the loafs of fresh baked bread. It contained cookies for kids under 12. The Cookie Club. Not to start there would have been devastating to toddlers. While I was a bit older than 12, I considered myself an honorary Cookie Club member. Used to make the ex laugh when I'd say, "One for you. And one for you, and one for me."

Even the kids laughed.

They knew I wasn't supposed to get a cookie. Silly, Daddy.

Once the cookies were distributed, the shopping began. See, it was easier and cheaper giving the kids a free cookie to munch on. For us at the time, anyway. The kids were distracted, and happy. They weren't pointing at high priced items on the shelves. The ex and I could actually buy what needed buying. And only what needed buying. Usually.

I shook my head. No time for memories. They didn't help. They clouded judgment. I needed to be clear. Ready.

"You good?" Allison said.

"I am. You ready?"

"All set."

We had a lot of ground to cover, with no idea what to expect. I didn't like it, and therefore, I did *not* have a good feeling about this. Not at all.

"Stay close," I whispered. The kid was practically up my ass. He breathed heavy. Uneven breaths. I knew he was scared. We all were. I think he felt especially vulnerable. A broken wrist will do that in a situation like that. He had his gun. It was just going to offer very limited resources if we ran into monsters. Way I felt, there was no way around it. No way was this store empty of those things.

Part of me expected to see long lines, customers unloading groceries onto black conveyors and cashiers sliding bar codes over laser readers before bagging the items. None of that existed. Might never exist again. I used to consider the process slow and chaotic. Never realized how organized a method it really was until now, with it gone. All gone.

We snuck past the scratch off Lottery dispenser machine, and customer service desk. I didn't see or hear anyone else in the store. Not even Allison or Dave. I was thankful Josh was in front as lookout. The closer we got to the bank, the better I started to feel. There might be a chance we could pull this off without incident.

At the last register, I squatted. The kid did, too.

"What?" he said.

I shook my head, tried to swallow. My mouth was dry. "You want to wait here? I can see the first aid stuff," I said, pointing toward the aisle. "I'll be quick."

"I'm coming," is what he said. His eyes shouted, "ain't no way you're leaving me the fuck alone."

"We're going to be fast, grab the stuff, then look for the others. You be my eyes while I get everything. Okay?"

"I can do that," he said.

I nodded, not a hundred percent convinced. I was at a point where I trusted myself. No one else.

The plastic bags were hanging by the edge of the conveyor. I took a few. Allison was going to try to locate a backpack, but she wasn't with us, so for now, I'd fill these.

We stayed low, bent forward as we walked the length of the conveyor toward the front of the check-out. I looked both ways, amazed not a soul was in sight, alive or otherwise. The place was a goldmine. Forget the produce and meat that would go bad soon, it was the packaged items that would last years that sat stocked on the shelves that had me excited. Figure out a way to keep the sliding doors shut, clear the place of any zombies, and we had a safe haven that might just last until the epidemic was put under control. Assuming it ever would be.

We made a dash for the health aisle. Didn't need to, no one was around. Once in the aisle, I snapped open a bag. I first grabbed bandages, alcohol, ointments and hydrogen peroxide. Then it became a free-for-all. Aspirin, Benadryl, cough syrup and anything else that looked helpful. I filled two bags before I stopped and listened.

"What was that?"

The kid's eyes were wide open. He stared down the aisle toward the beer coolers. "A ball. It just bounced by the--"

A small child ran after the ball. Arms out.

"What the fuck," I said and held my finger up to my lips to shush myself.

"She look sick? Like a zombie?"

"Couldn't tell," I whispered. "We're out of here. We have what we came for."

"But if she's not a zombie, how can we leave her?"

The ball bounced by again, going the opposite way. We waited. A second later, we heard a laugh, a giggle really, and the child ran past the aisle toward the ball.

"We're out of here," I said again. My heart thumped around inside my chest. I was officially freaked out. This was like something in a horror movie. Life was, actually, but this -- the child running back and forth, it was too much.

"We have to see. If she's alone, she's got to be scared."

"I'm scared. I'm leaving," I said, and turned.

At the edge of aisle, I snuck a peak right and left. Still no one. "Let's go," I said.

Nothing.

"Kid," I said.

I turned. He wasn't up my ass. He was halfway down the aisle, as if he were going to investigate the condition of the child.

CHAPTER TWENTY-SIX

"Kid? Kid? Jason!" I said. I wasn't about to yell. Why he was going to check on some child who more than likely was a zombie playing ball in an empty grocery store, was beyond me. It didn't make him a hero, just like wanting to flee didn't make me a coward. I don't think.

I cursed under my breath, tied the plastic grocery bags into a knot and hefted my shovel. Fine. I'd follow.

With quick, quiet steps, I caught up to the Kid, and tapped his shoulder.

He jumped.

"You scared the shit out of me," he said.

I wanted to thunk him on the head with the spade, but refrained. "Are you kidding me?"

He shushed me this time.

He was going to get a *thunking*. If not now, as soon as we were out of the store. This was plain and simple crazy.

We stood at the end of the health aisle. Neither of us saying a word. Felt like we'd been statue-still for hours. I knew what we were doing, what we were waiting for. The ball.

Only it didn't come.

We kept waiting.

I was keeping an ear open for Allison and Dave. They had to be close to wrapping up on their hunt for supplies. They hadn't screamed. Yelled. Nothing. I assumed that meant they were getting along fine. Gathering, as instructed. Ready to meet at the first check-out as planned. Unlike us. The Kid and I. We were looking for a four year old.

"Where'd she go?"

"To find her parents," I said. "We're leaving."

The giggle. It was close. Possibly. Hard to tell exactly where it came from. The sound echoed. Bounced off the emptiness of the store.

"Jay, I'm not messing around. We have to get out of here. The others are waiting," I said. No idea if they were.

He took a tentative step forward. I did, too.

We rounded the corner. The end-cap stocked with shampoo, conditioner, shaving cream, and anti-perspirant. I wish I hadn't tied off the bags. Those seemed like necessary items. Toothpaste and toothbrushes and mouthwash. All necessity.

"I don't see her," he said.

I worked at the knot on the bags. It made way more noise than I'd hoped, but came loose. Untied, I dropped the additional items in. A few of each. The bags became very, very full. I didn't want them to break. Maybe we didn't need the mouthwash.

"I'm leaving, Kid. You can stay. Stay as long as you want." I'd whispered, my mouth at the back of his ear. "Good luck."

I turned around.

Dropped both bags. One bottle of mouthwash must have busted. Green fluid spilled, pooling around the items inside the plastic. Smelled antiseptically menthol.

The child was four, maybe five. And dead.

Shoulder length red hair framed decaying flesh, and a frothy mouth with a missing lower lip. Milky, lifeless eyes were set below thin eyebrows, and long matching eyelashes. When she growled, upper teeth grinding against lower ones, I panicked.

I kicked out. My foot struck the child in the chest. She went reeling. Didn't fall, though. Her arms shot forward.

The Kid and I ran. She pursued.

We were running from a toddler. It made no sense.

It did. I couldn't kill her. I wasn't going to swing my shovel. Wouldn't.

"Run," I said. The Kid ran. I followed, but not sure why. "Toward the front of the store!"

He changed direction. Going right. We ran along the back of the store, passing the refrigerated areas. Hot dogs, cheeses, milk and eggs. Then cut up an aisle.

I didn't look back. Had no reason to think the child-zombie had stopped chasing us, but felt confident we were putting some serious distance between us.

"She behind us?" The Kid said.

"Keep running," I said.

We had nothing. The bags were busted in the aisle, and the whole purpose for entering the store was shot. "Run!"

I saw Allison and Dave. First check-out. Both had backpacks slung over a shoulder.

Maybe it wasn't all for nothing.

"Chase?" Allison said.

"Go," I said, "get out."

Allison grabbed Dave by the arm, spun him, and pulled him to the exit.

The Kid and I right behind them.

Outside, Josh stood ready, weapons drawn. His twin hand-shovels at the ready.

"What is it?"

"A child. A freaking zombie child," the Kid said.

Allison cocked her head to one side. "Seriously?"

"I wasn't going to kill her," I said.

"We didn't see anyone in there," Dave said.

"The child is in there. Hideous little bastard, too."

"Chase dropped all the bandages," the Kid said.

"You little mother fucker," I said. "I should send your ass back in there. It's your wrist that's broken."

That shut him up.

"I'll go," Josh said.

"No. We're done," I said. "We've wasted way too much time here. And for nothing."

"We got some stuff," Dave said. "Food and stuff. And a can opener. One you twist by hand."

I bit my lip. "Let's go."

"Give me two minutes," Josh said. "I'll get the supplies for the kid's wrist."

I knew it was guilt. Dave had broken the Kid's wrist, and I'd bet Josh spent his life trying constantly to right wrongs. "Two minutes," I said.

Josh nodded.

"And cigarettes. If you can find them."

Josh disappeared into the store. I started counting down.

"I'm sorry," David said.

Allison placed a hand on the ox's shoulder. They must have bonded on the tour through the grocery store. I ignored it all. My eyes scanned the parking lot. I saw a small herd of zombies on Mt. Read, but they seemed to be headed toward the Barnard Park, the Greece Police station--east, away from us.

The kid coddled his wrist up near his chest. He, too, was looking everywhere. His face was covered in sweat, his hair a mess. He was taking quick shallow breaths. I wanted to tell him just to calm the fuck down. Josh came out of the store. He held two plastic bags filled with the medical supplies. "Grabbed some toothbrushes and toothpaste, too," he said. "Figured, why not."

"You see the girl?" the Kid asked.

"No one."

"Let's head back to the woods. Bandage up the Kid's arm there. Then we can figure out how we're going to move forward from there," I said.

No one argued. Didn't suspect anyone would.

As we left the parking lot and entered the trees, the sky opened up. Rain poured down. The canopy of the trees was thin at best. Most of the leaves were crisp and brown and on the ground. We were going to get soaked, and cold.

Allison did her best to keep the bandages dry. She splinted the Kid's wrist, wrapped it, and then used the plastic bag the supplies came in as a glove, sliding it over the Kid's hand. She made small talk while she worked. "So are you a football player?"

"Was," he said.

"For the Greece Cardinals?" She pointed at his shirt.

"From the time I was five."

"High school?"

"Where I went, they didn't have a team. School was too small."

"I'm sorry about that."

"Was still going to try out when I went to college this fall."

"You're in college?"

"Monroe Community," he said, "they don't have football either."

Allison just smiled. Finished her work. "This should help."

"Thank you," he said.

I checked my phone. One battery line remained. I couldn't afford to let my cell die. It was the only chance of contact with my kids. Too much time had lapsed since the last call. I wanted to stay optimistic. These things out on the streets were relentless, strong, and hungry. They kept the five of us hopping. We were adults. Mostly. And fighting them off was a challenge. How were two kids. . .

I couldn't go there. To do so would be like surrendering. They were all right. Somewhere safe. Had to be. Had to be, or all of this--my life, was for nothing. Not a thing. They were fine. Waiting for me to come rescue them. They were holed up in a vacant spot, scared, maybe wet and cold now, but safe. And waiting.

"He all set?" I said.

Allison nodded. "He is."

"Then we're moving. Let's go."

"I think we should find shelter. Wait out the rain," Josh said.

I didn't face him. I didn't acknowledge his input. I didn't say a damned thing. I just hoisted my shovel over a shoulder, and picked up a backpack and started walking back toward the Tops parking lot. I wasn't concerned about who, if anyone at all, followed me. Either I had the four people behind coming, or I was going it alone. It was that simple.

CHAPTER TWENTY-SEVEN

The sky was not cooperating. It looked black. A reflection of our mood, no doubt. The wind picked up. The rain continued to fall. Hard. It came down at an angle. At us. The cold drops stung exposed flesh. My skin felt clammy, and numb. Drops dripped from my hair into my eyes. I gave up wiping it away and just pushed through it, squinting to see.

The good thing, the best thing about the weather, the zombies didn't seem to care for it much either. We'd gone two blocks without seeing a single one. It felt a little promising. Misleading perhaps, but I was thankful for the reprieve.

Dave and Josh talked in mumbled whispers behind me. No clue what the subject might be. Had my guesses. A coup? Go their own way? Whatever. It wasn't my concern. I felt like I'd be less of a target, and better off on my own than in a group. I didn't need, or ask for friends. I only wanted my kids. Nothing else. Once I had them, we'd survive together. The three of us, and Allison if she wanted to stay. That was fine with me.

When thunder boomed and lightning split the sky--a skeletal hand finger-stepping across black clouds, we stopped.

"This isn't going to let up, Chase," Allison said. Her lips had turned blue, teeth chattered. She shivered so badly, her shoulders shook.

I couldn't look much different, any better. I looked at the others. Out here, it smelled like worms.

I never asked to be in charge, a leader. I looked at the pooling rain on the pavement. My dress shoes were ruined, my socks soaked, my feet like ice. We were going to get sick. The lot of us. Pneumonia, or worse.

"We can't stop. We're getting closer."

"I know we are. I'm not saying we stop. Just -- maybe we find another house. Throw our clothes into a dryer for a bit. Find new clothes. Maybe we find an umbrella or two, and then keep going. We don't have to, I'm just saying," she said.

I looked down the road. We were close to my ex's house, but not so close. I hated that. "We are going to find another car," I said. "Roads aren't as cluttered around here. I think we'll make better time then. It will get us out of the rain. Turn the heat on."

"A car. Good idea," she said. It was a compromise, I'll admit. She wasn't going to push the issue further. I wasn't going house hunting. Not anymore. Not because of rain. Not because we were cold. A car, that was different.

"Keys are probably in them," Dave said. Hadn't realized he'd been listening. He pointed at the cars in the street.

Figure the people *turned* on their way to and from places. Climbed out of their cars, feeling sick. And then zombie-walked away. Keys in the ignition.

Problem was, the cars left running were out of gas.

I didn't hear a single car engine.

Wouldn't. Not with the wind and rain.

"Let's check them," I said. "Be careful. They might not be empty."

The street was ours. Zombies were not digging the rain one bit. Far as I was concerned, let it keep raining. It gave us time. We would be able to get further without having to hide from monsters anxious to devour our meat.

There were plenty of cars in the street. They were everywhere. Doors open on some, closed on others. They did congest the roads. Driving was still not going to be easy. I had no issue with riding on sidewalks and through lawns. "We want a truck, SUV. Something with four-by-four if possible," I said.

Fuck beggars can't be choosers. I wasn't begging. I was particular.

We walked north down Mt. Read. It should be simple. Pick a truck, look for keys, check the fuel gage, go. It wasn't. For whatever reason, there were few SUVs. The ones we came upon had keys but no gas, or no keys. We passed a couple of nice cars. I ignored the muttering and under the breath cussing when I declined said vehicles. It was something durable, or nothing.

"Chase," Allison said, "let's take a car. Get out of the rain. We can stop at SUVs along the way."

I saw what I wanted. A Navigator. It was in the parking lot diagonal from Top's. "That's ours," I said. "That one."

We were walking in that direction anyway.

"It won't have keys." It was Dave or Josh. Didn't matter.

"It'll be out of gas if it has been running all this time." Again, Josh or Dave.

The Kid sprinted ahead. Well, jogged. Either way, he was going to reach it first. He ran with that banged up arm clutched to his chest. Looked gimpy. I wanted to tell him to quit babying it, to suck it up and man up. Now wasn't the time. I'd give him a few hours with the splint. But tonight, if he hadn't changed the behavior, I'd lay into him. Might not be my business. It just annoyed the shit out of me.

He reached the Lincoln, pulled open the door. He turned to us, gave us a thumbs up. Must mean the keys were inside. Then he stuck his head in, and next his chest.

When his legs lifted off the ground, and kicked at air, I thought, *Ah shit.*

"Zombies," Josh yelled.

We ran at the SUV. Our weapons drawn.

We stopped a few yards away as the Kid's body fell out of the SUV. Splashed onto wet pavement.

Throat ripped open. Blood sprayed. Allison screamed. I almost slapped a hand over her mouth. My arms felt frozen where they were. Hands wrapped around the wood handle of my shovel. When she started to sob, and cry, I lunged forward. Long, quick, purposeful strides.

I knelt.

"Hey, Kid," I said. I pushed the door shut. The thing was inside. It planted its face against the window. Bloody palm prints smeared the glass.

He tried to talk, but only gurgled sounds spilled from him. His eyes were open wide. Teeth covered in blood. Mouth filled with it. I smelled it. Copper. Death.

"Hey," I said. No other words came to mind. I hoped it sounded soothing. Not shaky, and scared, like I felt. "It's going to be okay. We've got all those supplies from Tops. Okay? Allison's going to fix you right up."

The Kid's eyeball's rolled up. Nothing but whites.

His body felt limp on my lap. Seen it in movies. Always hated it. Faced with it now, I understood. I laid my hand over his eyes and lowered his eyelids.

More peaceful, despite the chunk of flesh missing from his neck, the blood soaking into my work pants.

Gently, I lifted his head off my legs and onto the ground, into the red rainwater, and stood.

"Chase?"

"He's gone," I said to Allison.

She grabbed my arm. Her head hit my chest. Her body shook as she cried.

I should have comforted her. She needed that. Hell, I needed it. Instead, I pulled opened the back seat door and used my shovel like a spear. Didn't look. Didn't hesitate. I plunged it into the darkness. The spade sliced through meat. The thing didn't cry out, didn't moan, but it gurgled. It gasped.

I pulled back and drove the shovel into the SUV again and again, stabbing blindly. Each thrust hit home. It was like digging a hole. If the thing had been on the ground, I'd of stepped on the rest on the edge of the shovel and forced it through the beast using all of my weight.

I slammed the weapon repeatedly into the creature, strike after strike. As long as the spade made contact, I didn't stop. I didn't stop until Josh put a hand on my shoulder.

I turned on him. Rain blurred my vision. Heat filled my cheeks. I knew my skin was red, from being cold, and wet, and angry, and feeling guilty, and responsible, and arrogant. Because I wanted an SUV. Because a car wasn't good enough. Because the Kid was dead, and it was my fault. All my fault.

Mine.

I spun around, reached into the back seat, grabbed onto a leg and yanked. The hacked up zombie toppled out of the vehicle, plopped down beside the Kid. I used my foot to kick the woman's body over, and away from his. She didn't deserve to be next to him.

"Okay," I said, "everyone into the SUV."

No one said a word.

No one moved.

"You want us to get into that thing?" Dave pointed at the black Navigator.

The rain came down even harder. Didn't think it was possible. Felt like ice pelleting my skin. I looked down at Jason. The Kid. No. His name was Jason. Jason.

"Jason was killed in there," Allison said. It was a whisper.

I shut the back seat door. Opened the driver's door. Jason's blood was on the leather. "Get in," I said, ignoring protest.

"Chase," Allison said, "I can't."

I looked her in the eyes. "You can. You will. This kid, he died. He died so we could have this stupid SUV I wanted. We're taking it. We'll find gas stations that are running and fill it up. It's ours now. It's ours because he . . . because I will not let his death be for nothing. I won't. He didn't die for you. It was for me. My fault. Mine. Now, get in."

She stood there. I couldn't tell if she was letting my words sink in, or working up the courage to climb in. Either way, it took her a minute. Almost two.

Allison understood. I saw it. It was in her eyes, when she couldn't hold my stare. When they dropped, and she walked around the front of the Navigator and sat shotgun.

"Dave. Josh. It's now, or it's goodbye."

I knew what they were thinking.

The thing had been in the backseat, and I'd hacked the shit out of her back there. "I'm not waiting," I said.

Dave said, "Shit."

Then he climbed in behind the driver's seat.

"We're getting your kids. And we're going to Mexico?" Josh said.

"That's the plan," I said.

"Wake me when we get to North Carolina," he said. He made a fist, held it out. I bumped mine into his.

Josh walked around the back of the truck, and climbed in sitting next to his brother.

I couldn't help but stand there in the rain. I looked at Jason's corpse.

I just didn't want to leave him there. He deserved better. At the very least, to be buried.

CHAPTER TWENTY-EIGHT

The Navigator wasn't 4x4, but the tires and wheels were big. The engine was Lincoln-strong.

I used a hand to swipe away as much of Jason's blood pooled on the leather before sitting down.

The engine started on the first try. The radio came on. Static. I took a moment and went through the preset channels. Nothing. Hit scan. Waited. It rolled through more channels without stopping once.

Allison blasted the heat on. Hot air smashed into my face. Felt good. My hands felt numb. I rubbed them together in front of the heater, and then switched on the wipers. It was time to get moving.

The Navigator was a smooth and elegant ride. Beat walking, being stuck in the elements. I pulled out of the parking spot, and in the mirror, saw Jason's body.

It felt so wrong leaving him there. He deserved better. I stopped.

"What are you doing?" Allison spoke in a whisper.

"I can't," I said. My head hit the steering wheel. Eyes closed. "I just can't."

Allison's hand rubbed my back.

We had garden tools as weapons. What more did we need. How long could it take? How much better would it make me feel?

"Chase?" she said.

I backed the SUV up, put it in park and climbed out, back into the cold rain. I heard another door open.

Josh and I looked down at the body.

"Bury him?" Josh said.

I nodded.

"Good call," he said, and pulled open the rear door.

Together we lifted Jason's body. I took under the arms at the shoulders. Josh had the legs. The kid wasn't heavy. Light, but lifeless. We set him in back of the SUV. "Thank you," I said.

This time, Josh nodded. "Where do you want to bury him?"

"I know the perfect place, actually."

We got back into the SUV. I turned it around, headed in the opposite direction in the parking lot, to the exit on Maiden, and made a left. In silence, we drove past the police station, and made a left onto Pomona Dr., and a quick left into the ball field parking lot.

Up rights separated the outfield to two different softball diamonds. I checked the rear-view. Josh nodded in agreement.

Jason was not Hoffa, and this was far from a New York Giant's end zone, but it seemed fitting. Appropriate.

The ground was wet. But not soft. The cold temperatures saw to that. Digging the grave was far more labor intensive than I expected. We all took turns. Allison spent the most time digging. Couldn't get her out of the hole. She wanted to dig. Eventually, we stopped asking if she needed a break and let her work. Tirelessly, she drove the spade into the earth. The rain helped. About the only thing it was good for.

About three feet deep, she stopped. She leaned on my shovel. She was soaked. Despite the rain, I knew it was tears trekking down her face.

Dave held out his hand. Allison wiped wet, muddy hands onto her pants, took his and used it to step out of the grave.

Josh and I lifted Jason. We set him into the hole softly, carefully. I zipped up his hoody, placed his arms over his chest, the splinted hand close to his heart. That damn splinted wrist.

I knew someone needed to say something. I didn't feel qualified, or worthy, even. Anything I thought to say sounded cheesy inside my own head. Sounded forced and unauthentic. "I wish we knew you better," I said.

Everyone bowed their heads, hands clasped in front of them.

"I appreciate you checking out that stupid Navigator, Jason. I just wish it had been me that ran ahead. Not you.

"I'm sorry if it seemed like I gave you a hard time. Might only have been a short time together, but I can promise you, you will be missed. Remembered. I struggle with the idea of God. Right now, I pray I am wrong. That there is one. That there is a heaven and you are warm, and dry and happy, buddy. That's what I pray."

I waited. Maybe someone else wanted to add something. Seemed like a good five minutes passed, just the four of us standing around this obscurely dug shallow grave. The rain grim, determined to add misery to an already unrelenting few days.

When I was sure no one had anything else to add, I reached for the shovel from Allison. I stepped it into the pile of dirt we'd accumulated, and tossed it over Jason's feet.

That's when Allison broke down again. She didn't hide the fact she was crying. Her lips, pulled down in a frown quivered, and her shoulders rose and deflated with each sob.

Josh put an arm around her, and led her away from the burying, back to the SUV. Dave stayed. His arms at his side. He was silent the whole time I spread the loose earth over Jason's body.

Dave and I walked back to join the others.

I desperately wanted, needed a cigarette. I forget how long it's been since my last one. I'd been too preoccupied to think about it. The urge intensified though, didn't subside. I just didn't have any. No idea when, or where I'd lost whatever had been left of my pack. Seemed trivial, but I had to get my hands on a pack. No question about it.

It was late.

As busy a day as it had been, we'd gotten off to a late start, and that hurt us. Everything we did kept me away from my kids. From finding them.

And, yet, I was determined to find a gas station store for a pack of smokes. It felt selfish.

I got into the SUV. I put it in drive.

We had nearly a full tank of gas. The heat felt amazing. We left the ball field, and were back on track.

"Notice we haven't seen many zombies at all?" Josh sat forward, his head between Allison and me.

"It's got to be the rain," I said.

Josh's head nodded up and down, like he was chewing that idea over inside his brain. "It's possible. Be nice if they were just dying off."

"I agree." Allison raised her hand, like she was in school. "It's always possible."

"Just not probable," Josh added.

"I didn't say that. But we don't know. We don't know much of anything."

"No," Josh said. "We absolutely don't. Except one thing."

"And what's that?" I said.

"Your kids. We need to find them."

CHAPTER TWENTY-NINE

When we were walking, it seemed like not many cars clogged the street. Like the roads were navigable. Truth is, they were rough. We were able to snake this way and that. We made good time. I took it easy climbing curbs and driving on the sidewalk, and lawns.

The whole time it rained, we did not see any zombies out and about. This gave me reason to smile. It meant my kids, as long as they were okay, would continue to be okay. Or should be, anyway.

It's what I allowed myself to believe anyway, was something to hang onto, at least.

"This is the street," I said. I wasn't talking to anyone.

No one answered. The houses were big. Donald made a lot of money. My ex must have been drawn to that. Because the squirrelly bastard was creepy looking. Creepy as hell.

Allison had a hand on my forearm. Not sure how long it had been there. Was aware of it now, as she gave me a squeeze.

I maneuvered a self-made path down the street, around several askew abandoned vehicles. I slowed when I came upon his house, saw his Lexus was in the driveway, and her BMW, too.

I pulled in. Left the engine on.

"I'm going in alone," I said. "Josh, sit up front. I want you ready to get us the hell out of here."

"You're not doing this alone," Allison said. It was the way she said it. I sensed there was more to the words. Wasn't just about me saving my kids. I think I knew what went through her head. Was hard even to let the thought flow. If my kids were dead, she didn't want me to find them by myself.

She really was an all right girlfriend. I needed to remember that. I needed to treat her better. Getting this far might not have been possible without her.

I nodded. We got out of the SUV. Josh climbed into the front seat and Dave into the passenger side. My shovel felt heavy in my hands. I held a hand against my stomach. I thought I might get sick. I know I was breathing fast. Hard.

The sky outside was black from both clouds and dusk.

"You okay?"

"Wonderful," I said.

I peeked into the tiny windows on the garage doors. My daughter had chopped Donald's arm off inside there. I cupped my hands, but to no avail. I could not see a thing.

Allison was looking all around, making sure nothing was sneaking up on us. I was thankful for the second set of eyes. "Nothing?"

"Not a thing. Let's go inside," I said.

The front porch held a swing suspended from chain links. Two wicker rocking chairs sat on either side of a small wicker end table. Fucking cute.

The glass storm door was unlocked, but the main door was not.

"Have a key?"

I shook my head. I'm sure my ex had a spare hidden somewhere. Think the kids even told me about it. Might have said it was under one of the rocks along the landscape on the side of the house. Kicking in the door would feel so much more satisfying.

I held the glass door open. "Hold this," I said.

Allison stood next to the door, keeping it open, and out of the way.

I backed up a few steps, and then threw my shoulder into the door. Fucker was solid. I tried again. Realized it wasn't the door that was going to give, but the frame. My third attempt shattered wood inside the house. The fourth time, we were in. The whole door collapsed into their foyer.

It was my first time in the house. Was I bitter? Spiteful? Sure as shit. So when I came for the kids, I waited in the driveway. I honked my horn. I sat waiting for them, swearing and cursing the very foundation of the tiny mansion. Now that I was inside, I hated Donald more. The foyer was huge. Large tiles, antique artifacts on display, and a chandelier. A fucking chandelier.

Money can buy you anything it wants. Even happiness. The old cliché was shit. He bought my family. He bought my happiness from me. Not stole it. Bought it. It made my ex a tramp in my eyes. Worthless. And he bought her with his money as well. Kids might not see it. Might not understand it. Eventually they would. They would know their mom actually walked away from her family because her husband -- me -- was tired, and worn out from working to support everyone. Fuck her.

"Charlene? Cash?" Yeah. I yelled. "Charlene? Cash?"

Something fell over somewhere upstairs. I looked at Allison. She'd heard it too. I took the stairs two at a time. My shovel out in front of me.

The house was dark. I tried the light switch at the top of the stairs. Didn't expect them to work. Not sure why. The lights came on, felt like sun rays exploding from the ceiling.

Five rooms. Guessed three were bedrooms. One a bathroom. Maybe the fifth a linen closet. That door -- to what I guessed was a linen closet, was closed. The others, open.

"You stay right here," I said. She could defend the stairs. "Nothing comes up. Nothing goes down."

She nodded. "Got it."

The upstairs hallway was wide. Two doors on the right, two on the left. The one straight ahead was the bathroom. I saw the shower curtain.

Way I saw it, three options existed. Two I could handle. It was either Donald or Julie in one of these rooms. I had no problem killing them. The third option was that it was my kids hiding. That one didn't make sense, Charlene had said they'd fled.

Confident, I strode toward the first door. There was an odor that assaulted my nostrils. Shit, and piss, and decay. My face crinkled, a failed attempt at protecting my nose. I looked back at Allison.

"Wait there." I just mouthed the words. The element of surprise, and all of that.

I sucked in a deep breath and held it. Entering the room, I tried to be ready. The shovel, what I've come to think of as my wide-point bladed spear, set to kill, not stun.

Julie was in the first bedroom. Must have been Charlene's. Even with her back to me, I knew it was Julie. She sat on the bed. I saw the edge of a picture frame in her hand.

"Julie?" I said. It might as well have been mouthed, too. I didn't even hear me. Swallowing did nothing. My throat was that dry. I tried again; it was spat out in a loud whisper, "Julie!"

Her head pivoted, first to the right -- to stare at the wall, then slowly toward me.

I was at the foot of the bed. Don't remember walking into the room.

The picture in her hand was of our kids, and us. A 4th of July picnic, when the two were much younger. In matching U.S. flag shirts, we surrounded the base of a tree. Cash on my knee, Charlene standing between Julie and me. All smiles.

Julie's eyes were flat and lifeless now. A clump of hair was *chunked* out of her skull. A creamy white foam crested her lower lip and poured down her chin. Long sticky-looking strands of saliva stretched from her chin to her chest. She was not taking good care of herself at all.

In a two-handed grip, I raised my shovel, ready to spike it down into her face.

She didn't move though. Didn't come at me. She didn't do a thing except look back down at the picture in the frame.

I'd not of believed these things still possessed anything human in them before now. I thought they were gone. Whatever disease had entered them had destroyed their innards and spoiled the soul.

This time when I swallowed, I felt plenty slide down my throat. It was not what I'd expected.

"Chase?"

Was Allison really yelling for me?

Julie's head turned again, looking past me toward the open door. The picture frame dropped. A hollow sound of wood frame on hardwood floors, and the quick *splack* of glass spider-webbing all at once.

In an instant, Julie was on all fours on the bed, and like a wolf, charging for the opened door.

I had a mere second to register the attack about to happen, and swung downward with the shovel. The sheet-steel flattened her out on the mattress. When her arms rose, fists planted, she pushed herself up. I battered her with the shovel a second time.

"Chase," Allison said.

"Kinda preoccupied," I said.

I spun the shovel 90 degrees, so that the spade was no longer flat when I swung downward at her head. It was perpendicular. Although it did not slice through the back of her neck, it did cut in deep. The blood did not spray, but oozed.

I hacked at her neck repeatedly until the most of the spine was severed, and her head hung dangling by some skin and muscle off the side of the bed.

She wasn't dead. Her hand still moved. Her fingers rolled into fists, and unrolled, and rolled again. She was not a threat. She would not sneak up on anyone, if she'd ever managed to get off the mattress and out of the house. If anything, she was now dying. It might turn out to be a slow and painfully agonizing death, I couldn't know for sure. I didn't know the science behind their make-up. I left the bedroom and closed the door.

"One down," I said.

Allison was not at the top of the stairs.

I ran into the second bedroom. Cash's. It was done up with Star Wars memorabilia. Action figures on shelving, and posters from all the movies. The bedspread and curtains depicted famous light saber battle scenes from the different movies. Hated to admit, but happy for my son. It was an awesome room. Beat the bunk beds I had in my apartment for him and his sister to share.

I went to the next room. The master bedroom. "Allison?"

I ignored the queen sized sleigh bed, the expensive dressers, and vanity. I hated the slippers by the bed, and the robes hanging on a coat rack in the corner. The wall mounted flat screen television was nice. I used the wood handle to smash the screen as I checked the closets and the bathroom.

No one.

In the hallway, I stuck my head into that bathroom -- and found nothing. "Allison?"

I pulled open the hall closet, just to be sure. Neatly folded towels, extra sheets, and bathroom supplies filled the shelves.

I ran down the hall, past the doors without pause, and down the stairs. At the bottom of the last step, I stopped, and listened.

"Allison?" I whispered. "Alley?"

A dish broke. No mistaking that sound. I went right, toward what I assumed to be the kitchen. Through the dining room, I saw a standoff. Allison held her hedge clippers closed, like a two-handled sword. She thrust the weapon out and at Donald, the one-handed asshole.

I hate to say this is going to be fun, but I'd be lying otherwise.

"Hey, Donny," I said, "you go after my kids, huh? You try to eat my kids?"

Donald turned his head. My voice was more interesting than the threat Allison posed.

"That's right," I said. "Here I am. I'd love for you to come and get me."

He stepped around the kitchen island. I hated the hanging pots and pans. The whole kitchen decor sucked. The tiled back splash, and chrome appliances. The marble counter tops were horrendous. Might be expensive, might be color-schemed perfectly, but it look like shit to me. I'd take my kitchenette, with apartment provided stove and refrigerator any day.

Donald lunged. Fast. Wasn't expecting it. Thought he was a slower zombie. Figured it was how Charlene got the better of him and why Allison held him at bay. I was wrong.

Like a linebacker, he hit me square in the chest. I reeled backward. Landed flat on the dining room table. A chair toppled over. I pulled my legs up and kicked out. My feet planted onto his shoulders and shoved him back into the kitchen, against the island.

Allison used a frying pan. Swung like Babe Ruth. Had his head of been a loose baseball, it would have sailed out of the park. Instead, the clunk to the skull knocked him to his right, into the side of the refrigerator.

I got off the table, turned, and flipped it. I dropped my shovel, stood on the bottom side of the table, and pried free one of the legs.

"Chase," Allison said. A warning.

I spun back to face my ex's husband. He looked so old. Decrepit. This had nothing to do with his being infected and now a zombie. It was just who he was.

"My turn," I said.

I swung. His skull caved as the table leg crashed into his ear. A tooth flew out of his mouth. I swung again. He dropped to his knees. The skull had cracked. I saw an overhang of white bone above the ear, and severed jawbone below. I swung again. He fell flat onto his face. I stood straddled on either side of his back, and swung, chopping downward. The leg splintered as it smashed time and again against the back of Donald's skull.

"Chase," Allison said.

I swung.

"Chase."

I swung.

"Chase, that's enough. We have to go. We have to go now."

I stood over the corpse. I looked at my handiwork. Don't let people lie to you. Revenge is satisfying. Fulfilling. It makes you feel better about yourself. Makes you feel like you came out on top. I took in a deep breath and sighed with pure gratification. "Let's check the garage," I said. "And the basement."

I knew my kids weren't here. I had to check the rest of the house. I couldn't just leave without verifying they weren't hiding under the car, or in the dryer.

"I got the basement," Allison said.

"I'll check the garage."

We checked everywhere. Behind, under, and around things. It was like I thought. My kids were not here. There was no note, no . . .

Phone charger.

I ran back upstairs, and into my daughter's room.

Julie was still sprawled out face down on the bed. A foamy puddle of spittle soaked the throw carpet under her face. That unbreakable string of saliva connected the pool to her mouth.

She moaned and groaned as I walked around the bed and snatched my daughter's charger off the nightstand, and unplugged it from the wall. I lifted the broken frame off the floor and scattered the glass away with my fingers. I dug the actual photo free, looked at it for a long few seconds before folding and stuffing it into my pocket.

I took the charger from Cash's room, too.

Downstairs, Allison stood by the door. "Everything okay?"

I held up the charger. "It's not. But this helps," I said.

It kind of did. I'd be able to charge my phone in the SUV. But if Charlene's phone was dead, what good would it do me?

Absolutely, none.

A horn honked. Could have been the SUV. And again. Then a car alarm was activated. Whooping over and over.

CHAPTER THIRTY

Allison and I charged out of Donald and Julie's house. Out front, zombies surrounded the SUV. They pounded on the windows, climbed onto the hood. I counted ten. Eleven, one was behind the SUV, too.

Nothing slow or sluggish about them.

They wore t-shirts, basketball shorts, and high-tops. It was like our friends were being attacked by a high school basketball team. There was also a woman in rollers, and an unbelted baby blue bathrobe. The old man in briefs and nothing else, had more hair on his body than a Sasquatch.

If Josh and Dave weren't in trouble, if this wasn't really happening, it would be hysterical. I'd be laughing. Only, it wasn't really Josh and Dave in trouble. It was Allison and me. They were in a truck. Locked away safe. We were out in the open.

I unclipped my radio. "Josh. Dave. Guys, get out of here. We'll go back in the house. Come back for us later," I said. I put an arm in front of Allison, swept her behind me, back into the house.

"Roger that." Dave's voice was crisp and clear over the radio.

The horn honked and honked as Josh backed out of the driveway.

At first I thought, what the hell is he doing? I realized then that he was drawing their attention. Keeping the zombies occupied. Saving Allison and me. Or, at the very least, buying time.

I locked the door, watched the SUV pull away from the house slowly, the zombies still on the hood, following and banging on the windows.

"What are we going to do?" Allison said.

"Be ready. Check the back door. Saw it in the kitchen, goes out onto a deck. Make sure we can get out that way," I said.

Josh wasn't leaving. He was bowling.

Once down the street, and clear of the monsters, Josh turned around and sped toward the gathered herd. Two things happened. Several of the zombies were hit, maimed, and some killed. While one of them bounced into the air, over the hood and smashed through the SUV windshield.

Josh braked hard. The SUV spun. Tire treads didn't grab shit on the wet pavement. The zombie on the hood rolled onto the street and into a yard, inches from taking out a mailbox.

"We can get out the back door. No zombies back there." Allison was panting, like she'd run there and back.

"They'll all be out front with the noise Josh is making. Wait here. Watch them. They get into trouble--yell. I'll be right back," I said.

I left Allison at the door, ran into the kitchen. And stared at the walls. I didn't see a place for hanging car keys. I checked drawers and all around where the phone was mounted.

Two cars in the driveway. Keys had to be somewhere. I knew when I got home, I walked in the apartment and dropped them onto the bookcase by the door. Along with my wallet and smokes.

I went back to the front door. Right there. A small table in the corner.

"What is it?" Allison said.

"We're going to be riding in style, I think," I said. "With the windshield smashed on that thing, it won't be any good to us."

Josh hadn't let up. His plan worked, and backfired.

I depressed the button on the radio. "Josh, all the excitement is calling more zombies. I can see them coming down the street from inside the house."

The SUV did a *thump-da-thump-thump* over a downed monster before the radio crackled. Dave's voice came through with static over the small speaker. "This windows shot. Front end is a bit smashed."

"I got us new rides," I said. "Allison and I are going to run out and start the cars in the driveway. You clear a path, come up on the lawn, and then jump into the cars."

"Roger that."

I handed the BMW keys to Allison. I didn't want to drive the car Donald bought for my ex. I'd rather drive his. Planned to beat the shit out of it after we got where we needed getting to.

"Where are we going?" Allison said.

It was an obvious question. My kids weren't here. The whole journey had been about finding them, coming to their rescue. Getting us back together.

They weren't here, and there was no indication to where they may have . . .

It hit me. There was one obvious place my kids might head to if things went bad at their mom's home. And it was safe to say things went bad. Very bad.

The solution was almost too daunting, too much to comprehend. I thought I knew where my kids were, or where they were headed. "We're going to run to the cars," I said. "Get in. Start them up, okay?"

Allison nodded.

The zombies were preoccupied with the SUV. Josh was unleashing a solid case of whup-ass on them, breaking legs, and rolling over skulls. With the new arrivals, there were still about seven or eight zombies. The guy in the whitey-*tighties* was down. His head so flat I thought I saw tire tracks across his skin.

"On three," I said. I placed a hand on my pocket, knowing the picture of my family was safe, and it gave me strength. I'd need it. We had to head back the way we'd just come. No one was going to be too happy about that.

We counted together, silently. Lips moving. No words came out. On three, the unlock button on the key fobs sounded. Lights on the vehicles came on. We ran, climbed into our cars and started the engines.

The Lexus had a full tank.

I hoped the BMW did as well.

I used the radio. "We're ready for you," I said.

I gave Allison a thumbs-up through our windows, and we waited.

Josh had the SUV in the street. He slammed it into reverse and sped backwards. He took out two, the truck bouncing over and crushing their bodies.

When he stopped, I held my breath. All at once, despite wet pavement, I heard tires squeal and saw rain water spray out of puddles as the Navigator lunged forward. It resembled a bizarre obstacle course. He wasn't going around or avoiding orange pylons. He was running the zombies down. One after the other. He did a 180 and came up onto the lawn. The tires dug into the grass, but the ground was too hard to rut up the yard. The SUV slid to a stop alongside the driveway.

Allison threw open her door.

I screamed, "What are you doing?"

She jumped into the passenger seat of the Lexus. Dave and Josh scrambled into the BMW.

Josh gave me a nod.

I engaged the door locks, and backed out of the driveway. I started down the street and Josh and Dave followed close behind.

The Lexus struggled going over the corpses Josh left scattered on the road. The cars were not optimal for this, the way the Navigator had been. They would have to do.

"The BMW have a full tank?"

"I don't know. I didn't look."

"Use my radio. Ask," I said.

She took the radio. "Josh? Dave?"

"Right behind you," Dave said.

"How are you for fuel?"

"Full tank."

I nodded at Allison. Sounded good.

"Ah, Chase? Josh wants to know the game plan," Dave said. "You have one, right?"

"Tell him," I said to Allison, "My kids are headed to my apartment. We're going there. Back to Ridge Road."

Allison's eyes went a little wide. She relayed the message. There was a long silence. The radio crackled.

"Josh says, at least we're headed south."

CHAPTER THIRTY-ONE

The rain had stopped as we started south on the main road. I learned two things. The zombies definitely hate the rain, and two, they were not just dying off on their own.

Despite the darkness of a fall evening, the creatures spilled onto the streets. The variety of monster attire was mildly humorous. Business suits to sweat pants and a tank-top, to evening gowns, and bathrobes with slippers. Sanitation workers in green jumpsuits to fast food employees in striped Polo's with cargo pants and complete with a big M on the brim of their cap.

"You okay," Allison said. Her voice shattered the peaceful silence that until she spoke, I had not realized I'd been enjoying.

"I am just trying to get my hands around all of this. The world is no more. I mean, I always thought we'd have a big war. Nuclear or something. That would change life as we knew it, you know. There'd be warnings. Irate third world countries threatening attacks. We'd suspect it was coming. But this? No one could have seen this coming. Or, no one outside of maybe the CDC. It's just, it's hard to accept it. There ain't no other choice though. This is life now." I sailed my hand from one end of the Lexus windshield to the other. "This is what we are stuck with."

She put her hand on mine. Squeezed. "We're going to get through all of this. Find somewhere safe. Find somewhere to live on some isolated island, and just forget about the world."

The pipe dream sounded wonderful, I was afraid to admit that even to myself. I knew I was smiling though. Felt the muscles I hadn't used in a few days stretch. "I just want to get my kids, Alley. Me, them, and you. It's all I want."

She leaned over, rested her head onto my shoulder. "I want that, too."

It's weird what we wanted. Before this, I wanted my kids for longer than a weekend. I wanted to see them on Halloween in their costumes. I wanted to beat the fuck out of my ex-wife -- well, I did that. Now . . . now it was all different. I wanted survival, and supplies, and a safe haven to sneak off and hide behind. And I did want Allison with me. By my side. I did realize that.

"I need you," I said.

She lifted her head, stared at me. I took my eyes off the road. There was an actual tear on her cheek. Not a rolling raindrop that dripped from her hair onto her face. "You need me? You really need me?"

And then we crashed.

Through it all, as it unfolded in that cinematic way of slow-motion, the horn blared -- long, loud, constant, a *Brrrrrrraaaaaaaaa* that reverberated loose inside my skull.

I thought Allison had a seat belt on. She didn't. Her body flew forward. Her head smashed into the windshield. It didn't break. It shattered.

Brrrrrrraaaaaaaaa!

That was all I saw, or remembered as my head slammed into the steering wheel. The seat belt snapped me back against the seat. I felt the burn of the material against my neck and chest. And then, and then the fucking airbag ballooned into my face. Fucking Donald. I could blame Lexus, but I don't. I blame him, my ex's husband.

At least my nose didn't get broken by the bag.

Brrrrrrraaaaaaaaa!

What was I doing?

Sitting in the car. Thinking about the air bag.

My door was pulled open. "Chase?"

Josh looked panicked. "Yeah?"

"You okay?"

I didn't know. I couldn't tell. I didn't feel anything. "We hit that car," I said.

Josh moved away, went to the front of the car. The hood was busted into a triangle. He raised it.

Brrrrrrraaaaaaaaa!

The black Malibu was in the middle of the intersection. We t-boned the shit out of it.

The horn stopped. I think it did. My head still heard it. Wasn't sure if the sound was actually being picked up from my ears though.

"We have to get you out of this," Josh said.

"Where's Allison?"

"Dave's helping her to the BMW." Josh reached in. "Can you undue your seat belt?"

I nodded. My hands fumbled for the release. "It's stuck."

Josh fell back, out of the car.

A zombie had him by the shoulders. It had been a woman once. She wore jeans and a blue blouse. Could have been a teenager. Might have been a woman in her forties. Her face was so decayed, I couldn't tell. "Josh," I said. "Joshua!"

I struggled with the belt, pressing, and pulling. I kept my eyes on Josh, though. He spun on the woman, breaking her hold on his shoulders. He delivered a solid right cross, and then another. She staggered sideways from the blows.

Dave came out of nowhere. Dropped to the pavement and swept the leg. The zombie went down hard. Josh pulled his hand shovels and pummeled the face and head of the zombie until it stopped crying out in that sickening moan and all was silent.

"Nice," I said.

"He's stuck," Josh told Dave. "The seat belt."

"We got more coming. Sound of the crash called 'em, I'm guessing. That horn."

"We need to get Chase out of the car," Josh said.

"Never seen so many." Dave spun slowly around in a circle. I just watched him. Josh was across my lap. He tugged on the seat belt.

"Dave. I need help," Josh said.

"We gotta move, Josh. We gotta get out of here."

Dave was crisp in my line of vision. Clear. Behind and all around him was fuzzy. Out of focus. If those were zombies, those fuzzy images staggering forward, then we were in trouble.

I grabbed Josh by the arm. "Get Allison out of here. She knows where I live. Go save my kids. Okay? Go save my kids."

"We are getting you out, buddy. Dave!"

Dave pulled Josh out of the car. He grabbed onto the seat belt, set his feet onto the door frame, so that he was standing on and inside the car, and yanked.

His face went red. He didn't look like he was breathing. He didn't grunt. Or groan. Or yell. The pretensioner gave just after the latch exploded out of the latch plate. I was free. And floating. Dave hoisted me out of the car and over his shoulder in a single swoop. "Drive the car, Josh," Dave said.

"That was close. That was close," Allison said.

"You okay?" Dave dropped me into the back seat next to my girlfriend. "Are you all right?"

"My head hurts." Blood wasn't pouring out of the cut across her forehead, but she was bleeding. I reached for her. Lowered her head into my lap. I combed my fingers through her hair.

"Josh," Dave said. "Drive."

Josh threw up an arm over Dave's seat, checked behind us as he backed away from the totaled Lexus and Malibu. He dropped it into drive and side-swiped two zombies as we continued on south toward my apartment. "We need to get back over to Mt. Read?"

"Might be easiest," I said. "I live off Stone, at the Ridge. Behind that Rite Aid."

"I know the complex."

He maneuvered the BMW onto the sidewalk. The street packed with disabled vehicles, bodies and zombies made it impossible to navigate safely.

"I hate to say this," Josh said.

"Then maybe now isn't the time," I said.

"Things are bad."

"You hate to say that? That 'things are bad'? Sorry I'd interjected. Say away," I said.

"No. I mean bad. Like . . . Jason was the last living person we've seen in a while. You guys and Jason. That's three other people," he said.

"Most people were vaccinated," I said. "They pushed that shot at every grocery store and doctor's office. I know where we work they almost demanded you get it. It's what made me positive I wouldn't. Now look at us. Now look where we are."

"What's that mean?"

"Look at us. This is life, our life now."

"You think getting the shot would have been the right thing?" Josh said.

"Sure as shit would have been the easier thing, don't you think? I mean, seriously. How long are we supposed to go on like this? Let's say we do make it to Mexico. You and I talked about this. There might not be an un-infected area in the US. In the world. Who knows," I said.

"I said things were bad. I didn't say hopeless. I didn't mean to imply giving up. I'm just apprehensive about moving forward," Josh said.

"What the fuck are you talking about, moving forward?"

"Mexico, or Canada. Surviving in the elements. Looking for food. Hunting for food. I'm used to cell phones and movies. Driving cars and going out to eat. I never had money, but life wasn't so bad."

"We're going to be okay," Dave said. He clapped a hand onto his brother's shoulder.

Dave smiled. "I know we will. Guess I'm just thinking out loud."

"That's a fire," I said.

"I see it," Josh said. "If it was daytime, we'd of seen the smoke all the way from your ex's, I'm thinking."

Allison sat up. "That all from the houses over on Mt. Read. We must be a few miles south still. Has it been burning all this time?"

"No one to put it out. Houses are close together," I said.

"The rain? That shoulda helped," Dave said.

"It should have, but--"

A tire blew. Sounded like a gun shot, or an explosion. I knew it was the tire when Josh gripped the steering wheel with both hands and fought for control of the car, turning into the skid as we careened back onto the road, and slammed into, of all things, a black Navigator.

CHAPTER-THIRTY-THREE

Josh swore before he climbed out of the car. "I'll change it. Spare's gotta be in the trunk."

There was never a good time for a flat tire. This just seemed like the worst. Allison more than likely had a concussion. If we couldn't manage the flat, we'd be walking again. She needed rest. Not to be walking. I needed the rest, too. I did not have a concussion, but no point in lying. I felt messed up. My muscles were sore already. I dreaded thinking about the pain my body would feel in the morning. Stiff neck, aching back for sure. The last few days has been nothing but car accidents. Injuries and accidents.

"I'll help," I said, and then realized I was right and I was right. The tire had blown. And it had been a gunshot. I realized it when Josh climbed out of the car. I heard it again. That distinct pop. Only, instead of a tire blowing, Josh crumbled to the pavement, his hands over his stomach.

Dave screamed. "Josh!"

"Hold on, Dave," I said. I jumped up and grabbed his shoulder. He had been about to get out of the car. I held him back. "Someone is out there with a gun. If you get out, you get shot."

"I gotta get Josh!"

"We're gonna. Get on your belly. Lay across the front seat. I'm gonna do the same back here. We'll open our doors and see who's closer, and we'll pull him back into the car. Stay low, okay?" I said.

Dave seemed to think over what I'd said. Took a bit longer than I expected. Then he nodded, and did as instructed.

"Stay low," I reminded him. "You too, Allison."

She was low. Hidden from view.

I squatted. I pushed open the back door.

I saw Josh's legs. "I have his feet at my end," I said.

And they were gone. "Josh," Dave said.

I looked between the bucket seats.

"He was shot," Dave said.

He was dead. The bullet must have hit him right in the heart. The pool of blood soaked his shirt, but was thickest, wettest, all around the left chest area. I sat back some, and looked out the window. "Some one's out there with a gun."

"We're not safe just sitting here," Allison said.

As if to punctuate her statement, another shot was fired. My side window spayed rounded pellets of shattered glass all over me. . . I was not cut. I brushed away the pellets. "You okay?"

"Yes," Allison said.

"They killed my brother," Dave said. His face pressed in the space between the front seats. "Josh is dead."

"You need to drive the car, Dave."

"We have a flat tire. We have a flat tire and Josh is dead. I'm going to kill those motherfuckers!"

I reached for Dave's arm again, an attempt to stop him. It didn't work. He shrugged my hand away. He kicked open his door.

I heard a gunshot. Dave dropped to the ground. I screamed, "No!"

The door was still open. "They didn't get me," Dave said.

"Get back in the car," I said. "We need to get out of here!"

"How many of them are there?"

"I don't know where they are," I said, but suspected they were closing in on us. I had to assume there was more than one person out there. I also had to assume they did not have the best intentions. If they had, they wouldn't be shooting at people passing by in cars. We obviously weren't the infected, the diseased, the zombies. They didn't want the BMW, or they wouldn't have taken out a tire. They wanted us, or they wanted whatever it was they thought we had with us.

The car was expensive. Maybe they thought the occupants would be wealthy.

That was lame, because right now -- possible for a long while, money was not going to be worth shit as currency. Bottled water. Canned foods. Cartons of cigarettes. That's where the gold would come from. Based on everything, I had no idea why someone would shoot at the car, kill Josh, and shoot at Dave, unless it was for bad intentions. I looked at Allison.

If they were men coming at us, she might be in serious trouble. Worse than death. "Dave, drive the car."

"The tire is flat, Chase."

"It doesn't fucking matter. Get us out of here."

"I'm going to kill them. They killed my brother."

"They have guns, Dave. They will kill us all. We don't know where they are. We don't know how many of them there are. We do know they are dangerous and deadly. Now stop thinking about yourself and drive the car," I said.

Dave cursed at me, but he was motivated. He moved his brother's body into the passenger seat. It took some doing, but he did it, and then he climbed over him and into the driver's seat. "We're not going to get very far with a flat tire."

"We've got to get further away from *here*, at least," I said.

Allison, at some point must have grabbed my hand. I realized it now as she squeezed it a little too tight. "I don't like this," she said.

Sign of the times, I wanted to say. I didn't. It had not dawned on me until this point. I was worried about surviving the elements, not starving, getting somewhere zombie-free. Never had it crossed my mind, and it should have, holy fuck it should have, to fear other non-infected people.

There would be thieves and robbers, pirates and bandits, gangs and murderers . . . the streets would be dangerous night and day. From the living and the living dead. There would be no peace. No sanctuary from evil.

Evil would pulse like a heartbeat, thrive like its own virus. "Get us out of here, Dave."

"I'm trying the best I can," he said.

A bullet ricocheted off the trunk. "Try better," I said.

Then the rear window exploded as a rain of bullets *ping*ed and *ba-chong*ed off the car.

CHAPTER THIRTY-FOUR

The bullet that killed Josh had been a chest shot. He must have died fast. I'd wager painless. I'd never been shot, and never died, so painless is relative.

Dave did the best he could. He drove all over the place, making lefts and rights. He managed to get the three of us out of there, out of harm's way. We wound up on Ridge Road at Fetzner. A hotel to our left, a Five Guys on the right. The mall was further west, past the Five Guys. My apartment was to the left. East of the expressway.

I was anxious to get to my apartment. I knew my kids would be there. Waiting. Scared.

Charlene had a key. Cash did too. But I knew Charlene kept house keys on a Miami Dolphins lanyard, one I'd bought for her years ago. It was our team. Cash wasn't big on football yet. He liked baseball though. His lanyard was a New York Yankees one. He loved it. But he lost it. Regularly.

Dave stopped in the Marriott parking lot. They called it the Airport Marriott. Airport wasn't anywhere near Greece, or Ridge Road. It was miles south off Interstate 390, but whatever.

"Dave," Allison said. I climbed out of the back seat. I opened the passenger door. Carefully I lifted Josh out, set him on the pavement and stared at his lifeless eyes.

"Josh," Dave said. I looked into the car. Dave had a white knuckle grip on the steering wheel. His head banged against the headrest, once, twice. The third time he slammed it back. "Get out of the car, Allison."

"Dave, what are you doing?" I said.

"Watch my brother," he said. "Don't you dare leave his body here."

"Dave," I said.

"I'm going back. I'm going to kill those bastards. Every one of them."

"Dave, we don't know where they were. We don't know where they were shooting from." I didn't have a good feeling. I sensed it. What was coming.

"Allison, I said get out of the car, out!"

"Come on, Alley," I said.

She moved slow. One hand on her head. She was not well. The car accident we'd been in had shaken her up. I knew we'd both be sore in the morning. No way around that.

"Dave, if you leave, you are leaving Josh. Because Allison and I, we're not staying here. We're not going to wait for you to get back," I said.

"You can't just leave his body here," he said. "That's my brother."

"Your brother would not want you to do this, David. He'd not want you to go back there and get yourself killed."

"He'd want me to kill those fuckers."

"I'm sure he would," I said, "but not if he knew you'd die doing it. He wouldn't want you to die, to get killed."

"Put him back in the car. In the back," Dave said.

There were a lot of cars in the hotel parking lot. This car had flat tires. Lots of cars also meant, lots of guests. Lots of guests meant the inside of the hotel had to be crawling with zombies. I didn't want Dave getting so excited he made a lot of noise. Attracting attention was the last thing we needed.

"Dave, if you had been shot and killed--"

"I wasn't shot and killed!"

"Just listen to me, all right? Hear what I'm saying. If you had been shot and killed, would you want Josh to go back there and kill those guys for you, to avenge you?"

"Yes."

I shook my head. "No you wouldn't. You would know that if he went back, he'd get killed, too. You wouldn't want that to happen.

Him to get killed just to avenge your death in a no-win situation like this. Would you?"

"Would I what?" Dave said.

He might be confused. But he was listening. Meant a part of him was at least trying to rationalize what to do next. What would be the right next move.

"You wouldn't want Josh going back there to die."

"Of course I wouldn't," he said. "He's my brother. I'd want him to be safe. If he went back there to kill them, he'd end up getting killed. Then we'd both be dead."

I kept quiet. Dave was working this out in his head. I think it was all starting to make sense. He didn't need me pushing and prodding his brain. He'd get there. He'd reach the conclusion I'd been attempting to draw for him.

Dave went silent. His head lowered so that his chin touched his chest. "What are we supposed to do now?"

Get my kids was what I wanted to say, to scream. "We find someplace special to place your brother."

The cemetery was just kiddy-corner to where we were, go figure. Ridge Road Cemetery. It was on Ridge and Latona. We had the tools.

I never liked funerals. Burials. Today I was burying two people. People who, in the short course of time, had become friends. It was the circumstances. In a million lifetimes, our paths might never have crossed. But for the last few days, Josh was more than just a guy.

"We'll carry him over to the cemetery," I said.

Dave looked where I pointed. "We could do that," he said.

"Ah, Chase," Allison said.

I stood up. I'd been right. The hotel had a zombie infestation. Or did. Looked like they were filing out of the hotel's automated doors.

"Are you going to be okay to run?"

Allison nodded. "I will."

"Dave, we need to get out of here. I'm going to put Josh back into   the   car."

"We'll drive to the cemetery," Dave said.

No point arguing. I lifted Josh by under the arms. Grunting, I positioned him so that his head went into the car. "Got to help me, Dave," I said.

Dave leaned over. Grabbed onto his brother and pulled as I worked to get his legs into the vehicle.

"Chase," Allison said.

"Get back in the car," I told her. It did not seem like a safe ride. If it still drove, it would get us away faster than running. Possibly.

"We need to go, again, Dave."

He saw them then. "They are all coming out of there? The hotel."

"Looks that way."

Dave shifted the car into drive, and on two flats, we limped back onto Fetzner.

"Got to do me a favor, Dave, a huge favor."

He didn't look at me. He kept his eyes on the road. He kept his hands on the wheel.

"I need you to get me to my apartment. It's less than a mile. It's right past that plaza down there. Past the Toys R Us."

"I know where Stone Road is," he said, "and we'll get there, after we bury my brother."

Allison was on her knees. She stared out the back . . . could not say window. There was no glass left. She watched as the zombies that had been converging on our car, now aimlessly milled about since we'd left.

None of them had been fast zombies. Had they of been, I don't think this badly disabled wreck would have gotten us far before getting overpowered.

Rubber was off one of the tires completely. The sound of metal on asphalt was dangerously loud. We weren't going to make it further than the intersection. And Dave was not making a left on Ridge. He was headed straight to where Fetzner turned into Latona.

"Dave, please."

"Help me bury my brother," he said. "Don't make me do this alone. Don't make me drive around with his body in the car. I can't do that, man. I want to help you. I want to see you get back together with your kids. We're going to Mexico, right? I'm in. I want to be a part of that. But, please, don't let me bury my brother all by myself."

CHAPTER THIRTY-FIVE

The car was done. Had it. Finished. The rims rolled on pavement. Didn't matter. From where I stood on Latona, it was clear even an SUV would never make it traveling up and down Ridge Road. It was congested as fuck.

Dave threw Josh over his shoulder. Allison and I followed with the weapons. The cemetery gate was open. We walked on in.

I was anxious. Any spot of grass looked good to me. "What about here," I said, pointing.

"I think under a tree would be better," Dave said.

Allison touched my arm. It was meant to quiet me. I worked. Instead of talking, I ground my teeth. Felt muscles tighten in my jaw.

Dave walked to the center of the cemetery -- it was not a big burial ground at all. Less than a street block. Place was old. Full, mostly. But it was peaceful, too, despite the main road traffic on two of its four sides.

I dug the shovel blade into the ground. Stepped on the rim.

Dave put up a hand. "I'll dig this one."

I nodded, pushed the handle toward him, and walked to stand near Allison.

"What time you think it is?"

"No idea," she said. "Eight? Nine o'clock? Midnight? Not a clue."

I closed my eyes and pressed a fist to my forehead.

"What?"

"I had my phone charging in the Lexus." My phone, the charger . . . gone.

"Chase, I'm sorry."

I wanted to say we're going back. That I need to get my phone. That would not go over well. Not after my speech to Dave. He'd never understand the difference. Maybe there wasn't one. "I'm fucked, Allison. If my kids aren't at my place, if they aren't there waiting for me, I'm fucked."

"Don't say that. We're going to get through this."

She didn't get it. I wasn't going to argue with her. If my kids weren't at my place, I give up. I'll totally surrender. Because this life wasn't worth a shit before. Without my kids though? It's not even comprehensible why I'd consider staying. She did not need to know that. Not yet. I knew it. It was all that mattered.

There was nothing more to say. I had a plan. Find my kids and get us all to Mexico, or bust.

Dave was a beast. I leaned my back against the tree. I felt helpless watching. I wanted to help. Dave didn't need it. He removed chunks of hard earth with determination, and precision. He'd outlined a rectangle and was now diligently scooping out the center.

It would not take him long.

Allison grabbed my arm, pointed.

The shoveling was a steady noise. The shovel striking earth, scraping rock, dirt landing in a pile.

With no cars. No horns. No anything -- Dave might as well have been a police siren screaming.

"Dave, hold up," I said.

Three zombies were in the cemetery. They ambled over our way. I looked around the tree. There were more. Outside the fence, groups roaming aimlessly about. They bumped into things.

All of them seemed slow.

It was too dark to make out much. The streetlights were on. Must have been timer activated. "We've got to be quiet," I said.

"Dave," Allison said.

I turned around. Dave had stormed off. He held the shovel like a baseball bat. He went at all three zombies.

"Shit," I said, "stay here."

I snatched Allison's hedge trimmers and followed after Dave.

Dave took a batting stance feet from all three of the zombies. He had earned their interest. They moved closer, one sluggish foot-dragging a step at a time.

He did not wait.

Before I reached him, his back-up, he'd swung. A head flew off the one zombie on his right. The body stood, arms outstretched for a long five-second count, before toppling over. In those five seconds, Dave had destroyed the remaining two creatures. He drove the shovel blade into the throat of the one standing in the center, and then spun to his right, full circle, and slammed the side of the shovel into the skull of the zombie on his left.

Once that last zombie fell, Dave used the shovel the way a shovel was intended to be used and dug off the creature's head, stepping onto the shovel rim with all his weight until the zombie was fully decapitated.

I stopped a few feet behind him, bent over, hands on my knees. "We need to get out of here," I said. I whispered. Dave handled these three fine, but the sheer numbers surrounding us was not on our side. The more I looked around, the more I was noticing -- like looking up at a night sky and not seeing a single star, but then all at once you realize the entire sky is starlit. Only, this was way different. "I mean now."

"I have to finish burying my brother," he said.

"I get that, Dave. We'll come back. Nothing is going to disturb him where he is. He's actually safer than we are. But us," I pointed at him, at me, back at him, "we're in some shit here. We have no car. Once those walkers realize we're here -- once they smell us, we're fucked. Okay? Fucked."

Dave walked at me. His chest in my face. "Go if you want. I'm finishing the job."

He'd kept his voice down, but the anger and disappointment were clear. Not hidden at all. "Dave," I said.

"You don't get it, do you, Chase? You've made these last few days all about you. Where you need to go. What you need to do. I get it, man. I got it. Your kids are important to you. They became important to us. All of us. Even Jason was on board. But you didn't see it. Never saw it. Thought everyone was against you. Or that every one of us was some kind of obstacle bent on preventing you from saving your kids. Even the way you treat Allison," he said.

"You don't know what the fuck you're talking about," I said between grit teeth. My eyes couldn't have been open more than narrow slits. I felt my face grow hot, hotter.

"You think I'm just some adult dummy, some retarded guy that has to have his brother looking out for him all the time. You might even be right. I suck at math, keeping a job, getting by at most regular things that people like you take for granted, but you know why Josh always had my back? Because if anything, I know people. I have . . . had a ton of friends. Good friends. The reason for that wasn't because they felt bad for me, because I was slow, it was because I knew what it meant to be a friend. To put other people's needs before my own, assface. I think once you figure that out, you won't be such a dick all the time. You might even start to figure out who you really are. I think I caught a glimpse of you here and there. You're not that big a dick. Be nice to see someday, to meet the *real* you. Now, excuse me, I'm headed back that way."

His forearm swept me aside, and he walked back toward the tree, toward Josh's corpse, and to where Allison stood with arms folded. She'd been watching the exchange, no doubt. She'd want to know what was said. Someday, if we got out of this, I might even tell her.

We knelt around the shallow grave. Dave was a mess. His tears streamed freely. He made no move to wipe them away. Somehow, we'd managed to dig quietly for the better part of an hour. The roaming zombies stayed outside of the fenced area. At one point, Allison took out a female monster with her hedge clippers. Stabbed it through the chest, and then spread the blades wide like the jaws on a shark before taking of its head.

"My brother could have done a lot with his life. Could have been anything he wanted. I held him back. Because of me, he sacrificed all he could have had. I told him all the time how much I appreciated everything he did for me. I never let a day go by that I didn't thank him for sticking by me, and he'd punch me in the arm, and," Dave stopped, lowered his head. He brought an arm up and dropped his eyes onto the sleeve. "He'd punch me in the arm, and he'd tell me he loved me. He always told me he loved me."

It got me. His love. His openness about the love they had. It hit me hard. I closed my eyes. I felt like I'd been spying on an intimate and private moment between family. I didn't belong. Dave made it clear to me, and I realized now how right he'd been, that I was an outsider. Selfish. A dick. This wasn't about me. I was in it. But it wasn't about just me. I'd made it that way. Made it appear that way.

"I love you, Joshua. I miss you already. I still want you to be here. I don't want you to be gone," Dave said.

Allison moved closer, put a hand on Dave's shoulder. It was all the initiative he needed. He pulled her in tight. His arms wrapped around her. He had his face buried in her neck. I could hear the both of them crying.

And being the dick that I am, that I still am, I felt left out. This was Dave's moment. Dave's time, and I felt left out.

My apartment was just east of the I-390 overpass. We couldn't have been more than a quarter of a mile away. We were spent. We had nothing left to give. Walking even a quarter of a mile seemed an impossible task.

Dave and Allison sat leaning against the tree until they fell asleep, and I let them sleep. I kept watch.

For whatever reason, not one zombie entered the cemetery all night. Perhaps the smell of death permeated from the ground. Maybe that dissuaded their attention.

I fisted a small handful of loose dirt. "I don't know if you'd want this, but I'll keep an eye on Dave for you," I said, and sprinkled the dirt back in place over Josh's grave. "I'll do my best to see that he gets through this. He's a pretty good guy. He's taught me some shit. It isn't so much a favor to you, or to him as much as I like the guy. I don't deserve him as a friend, but, in time, I hope to. To be worthy of that."

"You mean that?"

I jumped back. "Are you serious right now?"

Dave was behind me. He hugged me. "I am your friend, Chase."

I almost shrugged his arm off. Instead, I patted his massive forearm. "Thank you, buddy. Thank you."

"We're going to find your kids, Chase. I promise you. We'll find them."

When Dave finally let go, I just stared up into that sky, at all the stars and wondered where on earth my kids might be.

CHAPTER THIRTY-SIX

When Char woke up, first thing she noticed was sunlight from the slightly parted curtain filling the room. She shielded her eyes with the back of one hand, as she threw off the bedspread and sheets. With bare feet planted on icy hardwoods, she shivered. She thought she'd seen slippers before going to bed, but wasn't sure where. Right now, she needed to use the bathroom more than she felt the need to search for slippers.

Cash still slept. It had to be after seven. She wanted to be up before daybreak and on the move. Something about the room must have tricked them into getting a good night's rest. Sleeping had been rough the last two nights. Last night was not only refreshing, it was appreciated.

Before Char could remove the desk she'd slid in front of the door to block it, she needed to un-stack everything she'd piled on top. It didn't really make the desk heavier, it just ensured things would fall off and wake her if anyone, or anything, tried pushing their way in.

As she pulled off dolls, snow globes, books and dirty clothing, trophies, a lamp and crystal unicorn shaped knick-knacks, she listened. It sounded quiet beyond the bedroom. No feet shuffled. No grunts. No moans. Most of all, no smell.

The dead smelled. There was no explaining it, and more importantly, no mistaking it. She often felt like a wolf when walking the streets with her little brother. Her nose raised, nostrils flared, head cocking from one side, then the other. She wasn't trying to see the dead. She was trying to smell them. Thing is, you see one, it's obvious. They don't hide. They don't wait to attack you. One spots you, you spot it, and you run. And they chase. And the dead can run. Fast. Hunger drives them, no doubt.

But if you smell them, you can avoid them. Avoid being chased.

Chases are bad. It's how they'd gotten sidetracked. The plan once leaving her mom's house had been simple. Go find dad. She knew how to get to his apartment on the main roads. The zombies forced her and Cash to find alternate ways the last day and a half.

In this house, whatever house they were in, she did not smell the dead. At least not upstairs. Not near the still shut, still mostly barricaded bedroom door.

She cast a look at Cash as she pushed the desk away from the door. By the bed, leaning against the mattress was her pick-head axe. It was thirty-six inches long and just under fifteen pounds. Swinging it was not a problem. Crushing a dead's head, simple enough.

Char needed strength freeing the blade or pick side once embedded inside a skull. She hated having to step on the dead's neck and yank every time, especially when more dead were around, and there was only little time to retrieve the weapon currently impaled in a dead's brain.

She decided to leave the axe. The house was silent. Cash would know it was there. If he woke up, he might even take more comfort seeing the handle of the axe near him, than his own big sister.

Char twisted the knob slowly and opened the door but a fraction. She knew the hinges squeaked. But only at about twenty-five degrees. She also knew the third step from the bottom at the edge of the hallway squeaked. Normally, she'd never remember either thing. Currently, knowing what makes noise, when, and how, could be the difference between survival and becoming dinner for the dead.

Once she squeezed through the doorway, Char moved stealthily down the hall, past the staircase, toward the bathroom. She stopped at the banister, and gave the downstairs a once-over. Nothing looked troubling, the front door was shut. The chain engaged.

She sniffed at the air. Stale. Musty. The house must have been vacant since the virus spread, since the vaccination, meant to stop the H7N9, infected most of the United States. That was how long ago now? A year ago? Almost two?

In the bathroom, Char shut the door. Protocol was broken. She knew it. She engaged the simple twist lock on the center of the knob. The wood door was solid. Old houses were great that way. Hardwood floors, gum wood trim, and when taking shelter from the dead, solid doors. Nice.

If Cash ever went to the bathroom alone, she'd knock him in the head with a Bible and hope some common sense sank in. He was nine though. A kid. Stupid, even. Forget the fact he's a boy, and boys just don't think things through. At fourteen, Char knew better.

Usually.

Except this time.

When she finished with the toilet. She depressed the handle. It flushed. The bowl filled, her waste swirled and sank and shot through the plumbing.

Running water.

She closed her eyes, shook her head.

When she opened them, she knew what she'd see. The drawn shower curtain. How long had it been since she'd bathed? Just two days?

It couldn't hurt. A fast shower. Even if the water was icy cold. The idea of a bar of soap ... wait, wait ... she parted the curtain, and yes, yes, soap, shampoo – conditioner, a razor! A razor!

She had to do it. A fast shower. And Cash could take one too. God knows he smelled raw. She must, too, it was just harder to admit. Easier to blame the stank on him.

She stepped out of her clothing, turned on the faucet and almost cried. Water flowed. But not just cold. Hot, too. She was going to have a hot shower. It felt like Christmas. The smile she wore felt so wide the corners of her mouth already began to ache. The muscles rarely used, were flabby and out of shape. She'd have to try smiling more, just wasn't much these days' worth smiling over. She missed living with her dad, her parents being apart, and now this . . . zombies.

While it felt like it was over in moments, Char knew she must have been in the shower for over half an hour. The hot water was barely tepid. If Cash was going to shower, he'd at least need water that wasn't freezing. Or else she could just imagine him arguing with her about even getting in. And he was going to shower. Icy cold water, or not. The boy needed soap embedded in his skin, if not a flea-bath dip to boot.

She towel dried, pulled her newly scented Rain Forest hair under her nose and breathed it in. She didn't know if the dead would smell her, the way she smelled them, but she also knew the fresh, clean hair would only last the day. By tomorrow, she'd begin to stink again. And so would Cash.

Char decided she'd put the bathroom supplies into her back-pack. Take the items with them. She wasn't sure an actual rain forest smelled like this shampoo, but she was sure . . .

She took in a quick breath, lips closed tight and sniffed.

She released her hair, let it fall over her shoulder and turned her head toward the closed bathroom door. She sniffed again.

Her heart beat accelerated.

Dead.

Outside the door? Could be downstairs still. The smell, however, was strong enough to make her think—

Cash!

She spun around. The axe—she'd left her father's weapon in the bedroom. Cash knew how to use it. It was heavy for him, but he was getting better at wielding it.

The sink counter-top held a bar of soap, a cup with three toothbrushes, and a can of shaving cream.

With freshly shaved legs forgotten, Char opened the medicine cabinet. Pill bottles, creams, disposable Bic Razors. Nothing she could see working as an effective tool to fight the dead.

Under the sink, she found only one thing. It might work. Mostly likely it wouldn't. She had no other options. She grabbed it and unlocked the door. The solid wood --the only barrier between her and the dead-- was also a barrier between her and her brother.

Cash might still be asleep. Vulnerable.

She couldn't even remember if she'd shut the bedroom door when she left. She may have. But maybe not.

"Charlene!"

It was Cash. He was up. Worse, she knew that tone. He was scared. The dead had found him.

She threw open the bathroom door.

And screamed.

A woman stood there. Dead. Where the whites of her eyes should have been, there was merely bloodshot red. The eye was clouded over with a thick, grey film. The woman's flesh was purple, blue. She'd been dead a while. Whatever bit her did a good job at chunking out meat along her throat and shoulder. The worst was seeing bits of skin tissue stuck between the woman's teeth like chicken, or asparagus.

Char raised the over-sized can of Aqua-net and the lighter and did her best to mimic what she'd seen in movies. The hairspray jetted out from the small white nozzle into the dead's lifeless eyes. Under the spray, Char thumbed the lighter's roller to life. With barely a spark, the Aqua-net became a flamethrower, and caught the dead's hair and face on fire.

Dropping back, Char pulled away the lighter, brought her hands down onto the sink counter and jumped up and she kicked the woman in the gut with both feet, knocking her backward and down the stairs.

The hall was clear.

Except at the end.

At the opened bedroom door.

The room Cash was alone in.

A dead had just entered.

"Hey!" Char ran out of the bathroom. The dead turned to face her. She tried to light the lighter. While running, it was impossible. She dropped it, and the hairspray.

The dead raised arms and lunged toward her.

She dropped down onto one leg, as if sliding into second base, stretched her arms out behind her to get as slim and thin as possible as she passed between the dead's legs. Feeling a little like a crochet ball, she got back onto her feet inside the bedroom. Cash stood on the bed, the axe in his hands ready to swing.

"Cash," Char said, held out a hand to him.

She didn't want his hand. And he knew it.

Cash tossed the axe her way. She caught it by the axe head, and swung just as the outsmarted dead came back into the room.

The blade cut through his temple, left eye, and the bridge of his nose as if his skull had been made of warm bread. Blood squirted and poured and finally just oozed as the dead fell to his knees.

Char let him fall face first onto the nice hardwoods before planting her foot on the back of his neck and twisting the blade out of his head, ignoring the slurp *sound of the blade pulling free.*

"Get your stuff, Cash. It's time to move."

Any other little brother might moan, might complain, might ask for breakfast first, or to get to watch some TV. Cash was different. Times were, too.

"Where are we going?"

"Same as everyone else. Mexico." The virus wasn't there. The Mexican government couldn't afford the vaccinations for its people. Now, the walls our presidents built to keep illegal aliens out of America were being used to keep Americans out of Mexico. "They don't have the dead there."

"But what if some got in?"

It was possible. Probable. *"They didn't," Char said. What else could she say? "Come on. We need to keep moving."*

CHAPTER THIRTY-SEVEN

West Ridge Road resembled a war zone. The I-390 over pass had cars bumper to bumper, up on the sidewalk, and facing the wrong direction. Shattered glass, a muffler, quarter panels and a rear bumper clogged most of the street. In short, the road looked like I felt. My head was cluttered. My hopes so high, I was forced to rein them in, settle them down. It was, after all, merely a guess. I had no idea if my kids were at my apartment, if Charlene would have thought to go there. It was what I wanted to believe, that if she was going to feel safe anywhere, it would be with me.

Dave led us. He climbed on hoods, slid down them, and up onto the next. I helped Allison, lending a hand for support, as she'd hoist herself up and over and down each vehicle. Then I'd labor my way over, and onto the next. We had little left. We must resemble zombies ourselves. We moved slow and sluggish, with jerking motions. We were covered in blood. Josh's blood. Our own. We stunk of body odor, not death. Or maybe the stench of death was on us, and I'd just grown so used to it, I couldn't tell the difference anymore.

"I can't keep going," Allison said. "I just can't."

I could see Stone Road. Three lights away. We were almost there.

"Please, dear. Please. We're almost home," I said.

She stopped. Her arms flat at her side. Her head cocked to one side. "Home? We're almost home?"

I pursed my lips.

"Chase, we're almost nowhere. We've gone in a huge circle. We've spent days going like fifteen miles. Days. We've walked. Run. We've driven, and in the last few days we're only about four miles away from where we started. How in the hell are we going to make it to Mexico? On foot? We going to walk like two-thousand miles? We don't know that Mexico is even safe, that there aren't any zombies there. We saw that news report. The D.C. is in shambles. The military was setting up safe camps, but do we even know where they are? Do we even have a clue where one of them is located? We're in New York, and we're fucked, Chase. Fucked. I want you to get your kids. To have them with you. I want that. More than you might know, or even fucking believe, but home, Chase? Home?" She shook her head. She snickered. "I don't think we're almost home. I think we're almost nowhere."

"Guys," Dave said.

I turned my attention his way. I saw what he saw. It was a mob. No other word described it. We'd encountered gangs, and managed to get by hordes, but what was ambling its way east along Ridge Road was nothing short of a mob of zombies. If the wind had been blowing in our direction, I'd guarantee we'd smell them. No way could that much rotting flesh go undetected, even by the laziest of nostrils.

"I love you, Allison."

That stopped her. She closed her eyes. Her head shook slightly from side to side.

"We're going to need to hide, or something," Dave said.

"You what?" Allison said.

"Ah, guys?"

"I love you," I said. "I think I've known it for a while. I just couldn't say it. Wouldn't let myself believe it, that it could happen to me. I don't trust that emotion. Not even a little."

"Say it again." She smiled. Despite the mob. Despite the desperation of it all.

"I'm an ass, Alley. A fool. I could have lost you so many times by not telling you how I feel. And I wouldn't have blamed you if you walked away from me. Wouldn't hold it against you now. But, it's important to me to tell you now that I love you. That I really don't ever want to be without you. I'm in love with you." I stood there. Not sure what I was waiting for. She told me all the time that she loved me. It had always been awkward. I never replied with anything shy of, *give me a kiss*, or *you're the best, baby*.

Her arms shot up. They wrapped tight around my neck. Her lips puckered and planted tight on my mouth. "You have my heart, Chase. All of it. You always have. I've waited so long to hear you say it, that you love me."

Inwardly, I sighed. "I love you."

It felt good. Felt right. Telling her made my own heart skip a beat. Flutter.

"This is so cute, so freaking awesome. But, and maybe this is just me, if we don't fucking move now, we're, well, I guess, we're . . . dead."

I put my hands on Allison's shoulders. "I need you. I love you, and I need you. We can do this. Together. It's the only way we're going to get through this. Any of it. All of it. Okay?"

She bit down on her lip, nodded.

I spun around. "Got a plan, David?"

His eyes opened wide. "Me?"

"You. Yes, you. Have a plan?"

He tried to hide a smile. Not sure if his opinion, if his ideas or suggestions were often sought. It was kind of putting him on the spot. The more I looked, the more I realized the situation appeared a bit less than hopeless. We were on a bridge. The mob might be moving slow, but it was in our direction, leaving us little choice for paths toward an escape.

"They're pretty close," Dave said.

"And the plan is what? What are we going to do?"

It looked hopeless. Completely hopeless.

Dave's face contorted, he looked determined.

"Dave?"

"I'm thinking. I'm thinking."

"We're running out of time."

"The shadows," he said.

"The shadows?"

"Let's move to the right. Cross the bridge. Get into the trees beside the expressway ramp, from there we can go behind the Distillery, and wait until the monsters pass," he said.

I looked at the trees. Wasn't enough to call them a forest. Thick enough to seek cover in, deep enough to hide behind. Only problem I saw, was that the trees were on the south side of Ridge. Stone was on the north. We'd be headed in slightly the wrong direction. It was significant, though. Getting from point A to B was not a straight line any longer. The shortest distance was turning out to look more like a connect-the-dots game. There was nowhere to go on the left though. The exit ramp, the vacant restaurant parking lot, then Famous Dave's and Starbucks. Going to the right, as much as I didn't want to, made the most sense.

I nodded. "Okay. I like it. As long as they haven't seen us, we might be okay," I said, agreeing.

"Really?" Dave said.

"Really. You lead the way. You've done a good job so far," I said.

"Okay," he said, "follow me."

CHAPTER THIRTY-EIGHT

We bent forward while we ran. Staying low. Using the disabled vehicles for cover. We crossed the bridge that ran over I-390. Dave, Allison and I looked both ways before darting past the eastbound expressway exit ramp, and were in the woods. Best I could tell, undetected.

The leaves did crunch underfoot. A plus. There was all that rain to thank for that. The mush and mud wasn't great. I felt the ground suck at my dress shoes. Didn't care if they got dirty. Just didn't want them pulled from my feet.

"Help, please. Help!"

We stopped. Looked at each other.

"Where's that coming from?" Dave said.

"Not that close," I said. The voice, clearly a female, echoed. "Other side of the trees?"

Allison kind of shrugged, shaking her head. "Could be."

"We have to find her," I said. I know it sounded heroic, chivalrous-like. And it was. I did care. But her yelling was going to get all of us in trouble, too. Whoever was yelling for help had no idea what kind of swarm was headed in our direction. "That way," I said.

We cut diagonally through the trees, could see the end, only yards away. The Distillery parking lot was full. Just east of it were both an Applebees and Olive Garden. This small section of Greece was like restaurant central. And I was hungry. Very, very hungry.

It still seemed a bit funny to me that we stayed armed with garden tools. One would have thought we'd of come across weapons. Guns? Machetes? Harpoons? Anything. Guns had to be out there. It's all that was in the news as of late. Civilians and their personal armory stashes.

I loved my shovel, felt good in my hands, and now I had one of Josh's hand shovels in my back pocket, too. Dave's pitchfork was tough. He had Josh's other hand shovel. And Allison seemed to have mastered the multitude of hedge clipper uses.

We must have resembled crazed farmers scampering between trees and out into the back parking lot of the Distillery.

The woman still screamed. Not constant. Not always calling for help. She was clearly in trouble. Being chased, was my guess. We needed to hurry.

I chanced a look up at Ridge Road. We were at least a few hundred yards from the main street. Behind the restaurant was a Hampton Inn. Cars in the lot. From here, without the burst of cries and screaming, it looked peaceful. Not much different from the Marriott, just smaller.

"There she is." Dave pointed.

The woman wore a grey knee-length skirt, what once must have been a nicely pressed white blouse. She carried heels in one hand as she ran in the grass, toward Hoover Drive. A fast zombie in a dark business suit, complete with a thin black tie, was right behind her. He reached for her, swiping passes with bloated blue hands. She serpentined. Left. Right. Doubling back. Good moves. She was like an over-dressed running back. Her shoes the ball.

We ran at her. At the businessman. Dave had his pitchfork tines out front, ready to thrust them through the zombie. The closer we got to them; I raised my shovel, ready to bat his head into the outfield. Allison just ran, her clippers in one hand, not worrying about readying her weapon until the last minute, less it slow down her approach.

Just feet from saving her, the businessman won.

He tackled her, and tried to bury his head onto her shoulder. She let out a blood-curdling scream and arched her back and bucked him off her.

Dave reached them first.

He drove the pitchfork into the guy's back and hoisted him off the fallen woman as easily as bailing hay. Thick black blood oozed from the puncture wounds. Dave leaned his wait onto the fork, not letting the zombie roll over, stand up, or move at all.

Allison stood in front of Businessman's head. She spread the clippers wide. She got into a stance, one foot by each of his shoulders. Almost like eyeing a putt, she dropped the teeth of the clippers low, a blade on either side of its neck, and chopped. Hard. It did not cut off his head. It did bite into his throat, severed arteries. She repeated the process, over and over and over.

I held out a hand.

The woman took it. Her other hand was pressed onto her upper chest, just below the shoulder. Blood stained the blouse, where before some bleach and cold water might have washed out the dirt and grass stains.

"Were you bit?"

"No. It's not my blood. He didn't bite me. I've been in there, in the back office, locked in the back office for days now. Days. I just wanted to sneak out. Get something to eat," the woman said. She babbled. She shook. Shock, I thought. She's going into shock. "The kitchen was close. I'd done it earlier. Should have grabbed more food. I just took what I could carry. I needed more. The monitors showed it was clear. No one was in the halls. I didn't see anyone in the hallway."

Her name-tag read, *HELLO, I AM SUES MELIA.*

"Sues?" I said. I pronounced it like zoos, with an "S."

She stopped talking. Stared at me.

I pointed to my chest, and looked at where her name-tag was pinned to her blouse. She looked down, snorted out a laugh.

"Are you okay?" I said.

I heard it first. In the silence that surrounded us, it was like thunder.

"He almost bit me," she said.

She pulled at her blouse.

I stuck my fingers into the holes of her blouse and tore the fabric, pulling the sleeve clear off. She gave me a harsh look, brows furrowed.

"That was an expensive blouse."

"It was ruined, Sues. I just wanted to be sure your skin wasn't broken."

She opened her mouth to say something else. I held up a finger.

"I don't care about the blouse. Really, I don't. I just, you know what? I just don't want to change. I don't want to become one of those things. Because, you know, he almost bit me."

"But he didn't. I don't see any broken skin. We'll keep an eye on it. But I think you will be okay," I said. I had no way of knowing. I made my hand into a fist. Stop. Listen.

"Should I cut my arm off? Will that--"

"Shhhh," I said.

Dave looked around. Looked up.

Allison pointed. "There it is!"

It was the steady *thump, thump, thump* of a rotor blade. A white helicopter with a green stripe by the tail rotor. "Border patrol," I said.

Dave raised his arms. I grabbed at his elbow, pulled them down. "Wait," I said.

As if on cue, gunfire erupted from the cockpit. In the darkness, the bullets were like Roman Candles spraying all over Ridge Road.

Someone let out a *Hell Yeah*. Might have been me. May have been all of us.

"We need to flag them down," Allison shouted.

I shook my head. "Not a good idea. From up there, we probably don't look much different than the zombies. We should find cover."

No one moved, though.

It was awe-inspiring. The helicopter hovered just above the expressway ramp. Bullets rained down in glorious sprays that penetrated and obliterated the walking dead.

When the gunfire stopped, we *whooped* and *hollered*. There was a chance we'd beat this. Not just the four of us, but humanity. All was not lost. I swore I saw a rainbow arc over Ridge Road. Okay, it may have been imagined, but if one had appeared, it would have been as appropriate as hell.

The celebration was cut short.

The helicopter pivoted. The tail was degrees higher than the cockpit. It looked menacing when it faced us. It became threatening when it came at us.

Dave grabbed my hand. Tore Sues' blouse sleeve from my grasp.

"Run," I said, turning.

Dave jumped up and down. He waved the white sleeve over his head like a surrendering flag. He had the right idea.

We all jumped up and down again, flagging the air with waves of our arms. The piece of shirt made the difference. It was an intelligent sign. Zombies appeared dumb as fuck. Hungry, but brainless.

The helicopter stayed over the back lot of the restaurant. Suddenly, I thought running might have been the better plan.

Allison took my hand. Another sign we weren't mindless creatures.

Sues took a stance like she was ready to sprint at the helicopter. I took her hand. Looked at her. I had to yell to be heard over the spinning rotors. "No sudden moves. They'll shoot us all."

A speaker crackled. "Stay where you are! A Humvee will be by in an hour to pick you up. Wave your flag if you copy."

Dave waved the sleeve.

The front of the helicopter tipped forward, then lifted and spun around and flew away. We stood statue, still watching it fly north. I felt deflated. Help was coming. The chopper was leaving.

I still didn't have my kids.

"I want you guys to stay here. Wait for the military to pick you up," I said. "I *will* be back in an hour."

It was a lie. Mostly. If my kids were not at my place, I wasn't coming back. I wouldn't give up on them just because the Border Patrol was sending out a rescue team.

Allison still held my hand. She squeezed it. "Dave, you watch Sues, here. Make sure she's okay. Chase and I will be right back."

I wasn't arguing with her. I wanted her with me. Might be selfish, but I don't think I could handle being separated from her any better than I could, not having my kids.

"We're a team, guys. I'm going too," Dave said.

"I seriously need you to stay. Sues is in no condition to run with us. That's what we're going to be doing. Running. You need to stay with her. Watch over her. She needs protection right now. An hour is a long time. The noise that chopper made, it might have attracted more zombies than it wiped out, and you know what I mean?" I said. "I promised your brother I'd take care of you. Man, that sounds wrong. You are more than capable of . . . I promised him we'd be friends. As your friend, Dave, you waiting for the Border Patrol is the best bet. For all of us. We're going to do everything we can to be back in time."

Dave had a freaking tear. "Stop, man," I said. I pulled him into a hug. "We're going to be right back. Okay."

"What if you're not?"

"You got your radio?" He patted it, where it was clipped to his hip. "You tell me where the base is. And we'll come find you guys. Okay? Please, Dave. Do this for me."

"Take care of her," Dave thumbed a finger over his shoulder.

I nodded.

"Go then. Run. Hurry," Dave said. "Go!"

CHAPTER THIRTY-NINE

A vehicle wrapped around a telephone pole is the first thing I noticed as Allison and I crossed Stone Rd, and headed into the apartment complex. Someone was inside the car. Blood splattered the cracked front windshield. I couldn't pull open the driver's door. It was bent and crushed.

"Try the passenger door," I said.

"Stuck shut," Allison said.

I knocked on the window. "Hey, hey," I said.

The person inside did not move. Looked like the engine back was on his lap. We weren't going to get him out. It did not look like he was alive. I saw no signs of breathing.

I walked to the pole. It was split. The wires above kept it suspended. "Come on," I said. "Nothing we can do here."

Allison stared at the car as we walked into the complex, toward my building at the back.

My heart raced. I thought it might pop open behind my ribcage. I had no clue what to think. What to expect. I only knew what I hoped, and I was afraid I'd jinx it if I allowed even a hint of light into the darkness that made up my thoughts the last several days.

We stayed close to each of the buildings. Since the copter left, I hadn't seen a single zombie. Didn't mean they weren't around. They were. Had to be. I just wasn't in any mood to encounter a single one.

The nondescript brick buildings mirrored each other. Parking was a nightmare anyway, but right now, it was unnavigable.

Abandoned cars askew all over the place. Made Allison's words replay over in my head. Getting to Mexico seemed impossible, if only improbable at best.

We rounded the last corner, and saw two zombies milling absently about. We hunkered down. They looked like slow ones. What have since become my favorite. I wasn't foolish about it though. Getting overpowered by a group of slow zombies could happen as easily as getting taken down by a fast one.

"Do we take them out?" Allison said.

I made sure I only saw the two. They were it. "I think we should. Quietly."

It was, best I could remember, the first time we attacked them, instead of us waiting to be attacked. "On three," I said, smiling.

One. Two. Three.

We stood.

They saw us. They stopped. Stared.

We charged. No battle cry. Just with weapons raised.

They walked toward us, too fucking dumb to realize they were about to have their shit kicked out of them.

It was hardly a fight. I smacked the shovel blade into the side its head. It crumbled to the pavement, stood on its knees. I raised the blade above my head and brought it down crushing his skull. Goo oozed from its ears as it fell forward, face first.

Allison was pulling the closed blades of her clippers out of the second zombie's throat.

"Daddy!"

I heard it. It echoed.

"Dad! Daddy!"

Two voices. I spun around to stare up at my apartment window. Their faces pressed against the mesh of the screen.

I dropped my shovel. My hands rolled into fists. "Stay there. Stay right there!"

I ran for the door, through it, and up the stairs to my apartment. I threw open the door.

They were still on the couch, curtains parted.

"What have I told you guys about shoes on my furniture," I said, my eyes filled with tears, impossible to swallow the heart that filled my throat. "Get over here!"

Cash bounced on the cushion, into the air and wrapped his arms around my leg before I could even drop to my knees. He wasn't letting go, though. I had to loosen his grip. He re-wrapped around too tight around my neck. I didn't stop him, didn't need to breathe.

"Daddy," he said. "Dad!"

Charlene was beside me. She knelt, too. She hugged me tight. I fit my arms around them both. "I knew I'd find you guys. I knew you were okay. I never stopped looking, never stopped."

Allison stepped into the room. She wiped tears away.

"Get down here," I said, grabbing her arm.

"Hi, Allison," Cash said.

She messed his hair. "Hey there, Cash."

Charlene didn't say hello, but she did let an arm snake around Allison's shoulders.

# # #

I dumped crap out of my backpack. I snatched my phone charger for Charlene's phone into the bag, then emptied canned goods from the cupboards. I snatched some jeans and shirts from my dresser and the kid's dresser. The bag was popping-full, tough to zipper back up. I put batteries and my pocketknives into the front zipper area, and clipped one into the pocket of the pants I wore.

"I don't know what else to grab," I said.

The kids sat side-by-side on the sofa. Cash kicked his legs.

"I don't think we have the time to worry about it," Allison said.

"Where are we going, Dad," Charlene said.

"Away from here," I said. "Somewhere safe."

They both smiled. Allison, too. I might have been, as well.

"Daddy?"

"Yes, dear."

"I want to bring my ax," Charlene said.

She walked to the door. It leaned against the jamb. She grabbed the handle. The blade was coated in blood.

I did not want my daughter to carry an ax. She was my little girl. She'd endured some tough situations, no doubt, but I was here. Daddy was here. She was safe.

She was safe.

Or was she. Were any of us?

She had used that ax to save not only herself, but Cash, too. She'd demonstrated a strength and maturity, and courage that most adults never exhibit.

I did not want my daughter to carry an ax, but instead of saying no, I said, "Of course, you can."

CHAPTER FORTY

The four of us left my apartment. The backpack was slung over a shoulder; I held hands with my kids as we stepped outside. I did not want to risk letting go. Ever.

A hint of morning touched the western sky. Red-lit altostratus clouds spread thin across the distant horizon. I took it as a good omen. Right now, everything seemed like a good omen.

"We need to hurry," Allison said. "I have no idea how long we've been gone."

"We'll make it," I said.

"Make what?" Cash said.

"Help." I pursed my lips. We had been gone a while. We had over a quarter of a mile to go to get back. We'd make it. We had to. I could image Dave holding the Humvee. Keeping it there, even an extra ten minutes -- buying time for us to return. "We need to move fast. Stay low, and keep quiet, okay?"

Again, we stayed close to the buildings. We made our way across the parking lot, using cars for cover until the next building. At Stone, we passed by the car that was wrapped around the pole without stopping. The man inside had not moved, was still slumped over the steering wheel. I felt a little better about him being dead. I had no idea how I'd of helped him, had he been alive and trapped.

The plaza we crossed housed a pet, liquor, and toy store. Soho Bagels was a favorite of mine. Great coffee, awesome breakfast sandwiches. The sidewalks along the strip plaza were bare. By bare, I meant zombie*less*.

I listened for choppers. Heard none. Nothing.

We were making good time.

Getting back to Dave and Sues would be easy. Hopefully, once we returned, it wouldn't be long before the Humvee arrived.

"Chase," Allison said. Hated the tone she used. It shook in her throat. It meant she was scared.

"Look," she said.

In the parking lot, halfway between Ridge Road and where we were, five fast zombies ran at us.

"Ah, shit," I said.

"Daddy," Cash said. "That's not a--"

"Not now, buddy." I grabbed the door to a dental office. Too much glass. The front window. The door itself. But it was closest, and it was unlocked. "Inside, everyone. Now."

I didn't get this far to be eaten now.

Allison had the kids by the hand as I labored at pulling the door closed. It was set to close slowly. Hated that. As it shut, I realized there was no way to lock it. Was a key lock. I did not have a key.

"Find the back door. Has to be one. Go," I said, holding the door closed. "Move!"

The first zombie to reach the dental office didn't bother with the handle. Maybe you could blame the cleaning staff. I don't think he saw glass at all. His hands hit the door first. His wrists snapped back from the impact. His arms flattened, and then his whole front half slammed into the glass--momentum and all.

I took it as an opportunity, and ran. I sidestepped the front counter. Darting past hospital-green dental chairs, where large round lights hung overhead, I noticed trays of dental tools. I fisted away as many as I could grasp.

"Back here," Allison said.

A bell jangled. They were inside.

The floor rushed to meet my face. The wastepaper basket had been in my way. I knew it now, as I fell. My knee hit the tile. I winced, and gasped, and for just a moment, drew my leg up and in.

"Chase!"

In an attempt to scramble to my feet, I felt hands on my back. "I'm good," I said.

The groan and moan that followed almost made my heart stop. MY kids were feet away. I'd found them. I had them. And now I was going to get devoured.

The man's weight was too much. The small of my back felt like it might break. The thing had to be kneeling on me.

I released the handful of silver instruments, which made a clinking noise on the tiles, and snatched up the one that looked the sharpest.

The zombie had me by the back of the hair.

I squirmed and wiggled, trying to throw him off me. The backpack might have been all that saved me from having the back of my neck chunked out by a rabid mouth of teeth. I kicked with my legs as best I could. All I kept wondering was, where are the other four? Is this it?

Coming at me were sneakers. Jeans.

The zombie pulled back on my hair, my throat was extended tight. My eyes bulged. Not just from the pain of my head feeling like it was being ripped off my torso, but because the person coming at me was my daughter.

Allison was right behind her, running at her, but too many steps away to stop Charlene.

The blade of the ax dragged for a half second, before she lifted and swung it in one fluid motion.

I would have screamed if my lungs weren't being completely deprived of oxygen. I heard the *thwap* of the ax sticking into flesh.

The weight fell off my back. The hand that had me by the hair, released.

I was free.

I scrambled forward, my leg sending sharp shooting pain up my thigh to my hip, and down it to my toes.

"Are you okay?" Charlene was about to walk past me, looked determined to deliver another, possibly fatal blow.

I spun her around by the arm.

"She ran from me," Allison said.

"Let's get out of here," I said. The sound of glass shattering was so ear-splitting loud, I almost covered mine. "Where's Cash?"

"By the door," Allison said and ran with Charlene and me following.

Charlene carried her own weapon. I had no idea what had happened to my shovel. I had a feeling; I was going to need it, too. "Baby," I said. "Give me the ax."

She re-tightened her grip on the wooden handle.

"Honey," I said, "I need the ax."

"I need the ax, Daddy."

"You don't need to fight right now." I wanted to tell her she wouldn't need to fight ever again. I thought that might be a lie. She didn't need to be lied to. The truth was the only thing that would help us survive this mess. "Let me have the ax."

I thought she might cry. As she handed it over, her arms trembled. Possibly, she was happy to be giving it up, turning the ax over. The responsibility, and the stress and the idea of killing zombies lifting off her, I hoped.

"I want you to stay close to Cash, okay? And both of you stay close to me and Allison," I said.

Charlene stared at me. Tears rimming the bottom of her eyelids.

"Okay, honey?"

"I won't let go of his hand," she said.

"That's my girl," I said.

"We ready?" Allison said.

"We're going to stay behind the shops. Run all the way across. We follow the buildings in the 'L' shape and it will bring us out right where we need to cross at Ridge," I said. It was stating the obvious. I think I just needed to hear a plan out loud. It helped. Having direction.

"Got it," she said.

"Then let's go!"

The morning sun lit the lot. It should have been a consolation. It wasn't, it was the opposite. Easier to hide in the darkness. I felt we were too exposed. Too out in the open. Staying close to the buildings, running around green dumpsters, and cardboard box piles, made me nervous. I felt something was always on the other side. We never slowed though. We didn't use caution passing the potential zombie hiding spots. We flew past them. We had somewhere to be.

In bad movies, someone tripped, fell, and twisted an ankle. I almost held my breath as we ran, waiting for such a cliché to happen. It did not.

We reached the end of the lower half of the "L" shaped plaza. Here, we did stop. I held up my fist. The kids were behind me. Allison behind them. I checked around the corner. I expected to see at least some zombies.

I'd been wrong.

There was more than some. I counted ten.

"Chase?"

"Zombies. Ten," I said.

"Fast ones?"

"Can't tell."

"I want my ax," Charlene said.

I closed my eyes. "We can't go this way."

"We can't go back the way we came. We don't have time for that," Allison said. I wish she'd stayed with Dave. The Humvee would be there, or was there. She'd be safe. It would be one less person I had to worry about. "Try the radio."

"There's nothing Dave can do," I said.

"Maybe the Border Patrol is there, and they can help."

"And if they're not? Then Dave's going to come. I don't want him trying to save us. He has a chance to get out of this," I said.

"We all do."

I bit my lip and lifted the radio. "Dave? Dave you there?"

We waited. Silence. It boomed. Nothing.

"Dave?"

They might be gone already. Rescued. I lowered the radio; fit the clip onto my pants.

It crackled. "Chase? Chase, where are you? Over."

I looked at Allison. "We have my kids. We're behind the Toys R Us. Making our way back to you. The Humvee there?"

"Not yet. Over," he said.

"You guys safe?"

"So far. We're staying low. Keeping quiet. Over."

"Listen, you don't wait for us. Got it? You hear me?"

Allison reached for the radio. "What are you doing?"

I was saving lives. "Stop it," I said.

I knew what I was doing. My kids were with me. I wanted them out of here more than anything. I shut the radio off. "We're going to make it," I said. "Humvee's not there yet. So we have time."

Allison shook her head. "Whatever you say."

I ignored the poison in her words. Passive aggressiveness wasn't going to change my mind. Not this time. I was going to save us. All of us. I just wasn't sure how. Yet.

CHAPTER FORTY-ONE

So far, we'd made it nowhere. We stood, the four of us, with backs to the cinder block wall. Possibly only minutes had passed. Felt like hours. I kept checking around the corner.

The zombies were still there. They milled about. They were closer though. We'd have to move.

"What are we going to do?"

I stared at Allison, then past her, and smiled.

"What? You have an idea."

The sun finally worked to our advantage.

The daylight, you might say, had saved us.

I pointed.

Allison turned. She looked back at me. She was all smiles. "Let's go kids," she said.

I hoisted Cash up onto the Dumpster. It sat behind a Chinese takeout place. I couldn't read the writing on the back door.

Sure, we could have tried all the back doors into the different shops. I didn't want to be trapped inside. Who knew how many zombies might be lurking about.

Charlene climbed up next, on her own. She set her hands inside the slid-open Dumpster door, and planted a foot as high as possible, and hoisted herself up. She pushed up and stood onto the dumpster next to her brother. She held out a hand for Allison.

I gave Allison a lift.

Then I heard them. Unmistakable moans. Groans.

"Behind you, Daddy," Charlene said, as Allison and she clasped hands. I pushed. Charlene pulled and Allison was up. And safe.

I handed them the ax. I copied my daughter. Hands inside the opening on the sliding door. Planted my foot.

"Daddy!"

I knew they were more than right behind me.

My dress shoes slipped on the outside wall of the dumpster.

I turned around, and ducked.

The zombie lunged. He fell halfway into the garbage. I grabbed his legs. He flopped inside the Dumpster.

I had mere seconds to try again. I wasn't comfortable climbing the dumpster by the open door, so I closed it. I pulled myself halfway up.

"They're all coming, Chase. Hurry. Hurry."

I refrained from telling Allison she wasn't helping by panicking.

My girls lifted me by tugging on the backpack.

I heard Cash. He was crying.

I'd comfort him, but not yet. We had to move.

Once we were on the dumpster, the ladder to the roof was easy to access. Would have been better if the dumpster was slightly closer to the back of the building. We'd manage.

The gathering zombies surrounded the dumpster.

We had no way down, or out. The ladder, the roof, was now our only option. My face felt hot. I knew I was sweating. "Allison, you're going first."

She didn't argue. She knew she'd need to help get the kids over and up.

She stood on the edge of the dumpster. Fingertips of the zombies clawed at the toe of her shoes -- just out of reach from grabbing her foot and yanking her off, and down for their mealtime.

"Daddy!" Cash was shaking.

"We're almost there, buddy. We're almost out of here."

Allison stretched a leg out towards the first ladder wrung.

"I don't reach," she said.

"You'll have to jump to it," I said. It was obvious.

"I don't think I can," she said.

"Alley, you almost reach. It's not a far jump. Just keep your eyes on the ladder. Reach for the ladder with both hands," I said.

She clapped her hands together. It would be cute if she were working up nerve to jump into a swimming pool. Right now, I was simply annoyed.

"Alley! Jump!"

Startled, she jumped.

In my mind's eye I saw it. She fell. Twisted her ankle. The zombies were on her. Tore at her flesh.

It was not what happened.

She'd made it. One arm wrapped around a wrung at the bend in her elbow. Her feet dangled, taunting the zombies below. Except where she was, they could reach her leg. "Get up the ladder," I shouted.

She climbed. Clung to the iron. I heard her panting.

"Alley?"

"Piece of cake. Easy, peasy."

She either said it for the sake of the kids, or for herself.

"Okay, Cash. You're next," she said.

I grabbed Cash by the waist and lifted him. He squirmed. "No! No!"

I didn't stop. Allison held out an arm. The other locked around the ladder. I set Cash into her hand, and she pulled him to her chest. "Climb all the way up," she said.

He did, stepping around Allison. He stopped just as his head peeked over the top.

"Anything?" I said.

"No one's up here," he said. He finished the climb, and stood on the roof.

"You wait right there," I said. "You're next, Charlene."

I reached for her waist.

"I got this," she told me.

This was no time to demonstrate independence. Or was it. To prevent becoming an obstacle for my daughter, Allison climbed all the way up to the roof with Cash.

"Okay," I said. "Go."

Charlene made the leap from the dumpster to the ladder easier than Allison had. She climbed up and over.

Three down. Me to go.

CHAPTER FORTY-TWO

We stood on the roof of the plaza. I looked down at the dumpster. Thankfully, the zombies looked dumbfounded. They'd been outsmarted. Watched it happen and still couldn't figure out how to get up her to eat us.

"Dad," Charlene said, "how do we get back down?"

My eyes widened and I exhaled a puff of breath. Wasn't exactly a sigh. "One problem at a time," I said. I smiled.

We made our way along the roof, toward Ridge Road. "Stay close to the side," I said. Worried the roof might not hold our weight. No reason it shouldn't. Winters were brutal. Snow weighed a lot. But roofs also collapsed during winter storms. Why risk it?

We didn't need to move slowly. We didn't need to hide, really. We just had to walk, and made it to the end of the plaza.

Below us, I didn't point out, but noticed, were more zombies. Too many. I couldn't count them. We hadn't attracted their attention yet. I didn't think we'd been spotted.

Charlene was right, though. We were up here. No easy way down. And no reason to climb down anyway, not with that many monsters lurking. There had to be fast ones mixed in. They'd pick us off one at a time as we got off the roof.

I'd said one problem at a time.

It was time.

This was a problem.

"Everyone, sit," I said.

We sat.

I needed the time to think. No ideas came to mind. I pulled the radio off my waist. Stared at it. I strained to look across the street. Olive Garden blocked my view, as did the footbridge over Ridge Road.

I listened.

I did not hear any vehicle engines. No gunfire. Nothing.

We were stuck. Stranded. I had food in my pack, we could stay up here a while. That wouldn't get us rescued. It might buy us time though, until the zombies were gone.

I set my face into cupped hands. I knew I looked hopeless, but right now, I just was at a complete and utter loss.

"We're going to be all right, Dad," Charlene said. She sat next to me.

Cash came over, too.

Sitting on either side, they both put an arm around me.

It was hard not to smile at them. "Yes. Of course we are."

"There it is, Chase," Allison said.

I had not heard it, because it was not loud.

The huge Humvee was pulling onto Hoover Drive, headed toward Ridge Road. It maneuvered around abandoned vehicles effortlessly. "Will they see us?" I said.

We all stood. Arms waving. Cash was yelling, "Over here!"

The Humvee turned left.

Not right.

Headed west onto Ridge Road.

Not east.

"No," Allison said. "Where are they going?"

They must have a schedule, I thought. I touched Allison's shoulder. "We're going to be okay."

Maybe not. Our yelling had excited the zombies below. Agitated them. Possibly reminded them of just how hungry they really were.

We were now the blue light. The bugs coming at us from all directions.

I looked across the parking lot.

Son of a bitch, was about all I could think. Son of a bitch.

We were safest up top. For now. There were ways into the stores from up here. I just didn't like the idea. Not at all. For now, we'd wait it out.

"Get down everyone," I said. "Stay low. Keep quiet."

Cash had gone from looking victorious to crushed. His lips quivered. He buried his head against me. "We're going to get away from here, little guy."

We all laid flat on the rooftop.

Cash was pressed tight against me. "I do have a plan," I said.

Allison looked at me, eyes wide.

I winked, and pursed my lips.

Her expression deflated. She knew I'd just lied.

I needed to. It felt necessary.

"What is it, Dad," Charlene said.

"First, we need to wait for the zombies to forget we're up here."

"Will they?" she said.

"They lose interest fast, dear. Or they have short-term memory problems. Whatever it is, in a few minutes, they'll all wander off, toward some other sound," I said.

"They will?" Charlene did not sound confident in my assessment.

"We've done it to them before," Allison said, almost beaming with pride.

It made me smile. "Yes, we have," I said.

But would they? Only thing I ever seen them do was eat. Humans. Non infected people. They didn't feed on each other. Why? I had no idea. Made no sense. Way it looked, the four of us, up here on this roof, we were it. The only meal for apparent miles in any direction. If I were hungry, I wouldn't move from the food source. We were that source right now. Would they eventually all starve to death then? Would they naturally die off? Or would they adapt. Start eating cows and horses and dogs and cats and birds and vegetables. I had no answer to any of these stupid, stupid questions. We were--

Rumbling.

Distinct rumbling.

I shot my hand out. Allison took it.

We all rose to our knees. Cash pointed first. He knew.

No one spoke.

There wasn't a need.

The Humvee was traveling eastbound in the westbound lane. Less stranded cars clogging the road. The fucking thing had to make a U-turn. A fucking U-turn.

They weren't leaving us.

The radio came to life. "Hey buddy, hang tight!"

I held the radio in both hands. I stared at it. My smile was too big to hide.

"You're crying," Allison said.

I wiped tears from her eyes. "I'm not the only one."

We had to resemble flood victims, huddled close, arms wrapped around one another watching help approaching.

A gunner on top of the Humvee appeared. He fired into the cluster of zombies. That thick black goo that must be blood flew like popping water balloons. The creatures fell onto the pavement with destroyed skulls and amputations.

"I love you, Alley," I said. And I kissed her.

Cash clapped a hand to his forehead, but he wore a smile that matched mine. Charlene just hugged me, tight. Possibly a bit possessively.

"We're saved, Dad," she said. "We're finally going to be all right."

"Everything is going to be fine now, honey. We're going to be all right."

EPILOGUE

The Humvee was crowded. I had a kid on each lap, even though it seemed to humiliate Charlene. She was, after all, fourteen. Too big to sit on her daddy's lap, no doubt. I was loving it. Allison was on my side, sharing no space at all, and flattened against the door.

Dave and Sues sat across from us, practically on each other's laps, too. The gunner stayed up top. There was nothing more to shoot at. There was just nowhere inside the military vehicle for him to sit.

"We thought you guys had left us," I said. It was loud inside the Humvee. Not a quiet ride like Donald's Lexus. It was quite honestly one of the best sounds I'd heard in a while. I didn't mind.

"They wanted to," Sues said. "Something about a tight schedule. But Dave wouldn't let 'em. Especially not when the Lieutenant up front spotted you guys on the roof across the street."

"We were coming for you, if I had to take the wheel," Dave yelled.

The passenger in camo, and holding an assault rifle looked back at us. Even with sunglasses on, I read his eyes. *No Fucking Chance, Dave.*

Whatever.

"Where are we going?" I said.

Dave opened his mouth.

The passenger spoke. "That's classified, sir."

"Is there one of those camps nearby?" I said.

"Classified, sir," he said.

"Are there a lot of healthy soldiers? I'd just assume that most of you were forced to be vaccinated. You guys gotta get like every shot there is, don't you."

Silence.

I didn't like it. It wasn't that I was being ignored, it was that they weren't sharing information. Keeping us civilians in the dark. We needed to get past that. Work together.

"Excuse me," I said.

He turned his head. The sunglasses kind of annoyed me now. It all seemed like part of a mask.

"Are we staying in Rochester, can you tell me that much? I mean, we're not blindfolded, so I assume it can't be that far above my pay grade for classification," I said. I hoped the bite in my sarcasm wasn't lost. Doubt it was.

"We are not staying in Rochester."

"Thank you." I thought, "are we headed south?"

"Northeast."

"What's northeast?" I said.

Together, we said, "Classified, sir."

"Right, right, I got it," I said.

"We're safe," Allison whispered. "We're safe."

I tried to look out the window. They were tinted pretty good. Hard to see much of anything. We drove on, bouncing down whatever road--real or created--the Humvee traveled along. Silence ensued.

Cash's head was on my chest. Eyes closed. Mouth open. He'd always been able to sleep in car rides. Settled him down, and put him right out. Not Charlene. Not then, and not now.

"Do you trust them," she said, tilting her head to indicate the men up front.

I pursed my lips. Tight.

I shook my head a fraction, side to side.

Charlene took a deep breath, and sighed. She mouthed the words, "Me either."

THE END

Bio:

Phillip Tomasso is the award winning author of numorous novels, and short stories.
He works full time as a Fire/EMS Dispatcher at 911. He lives in Rochester, NY with his three children,
dog, Fettucine and cat, Luca. He is always at work on his next tale.

www.philliptomasso.com / phillip@philliptomasso.com

Other Titles:

Sounds of Silence
Pulse of Evil
Pigeon Drop
Convicted
The Molech Prophecy (as Thomas Phillips)
Adverse Impact
Johnny Blade
Third Ring
Tenth House
Mind Play